CHAPTER 1

*S*he had never kidnapped an earl before.

She had never kidnapped anyone before for that matter, and she wasn't sure if it was exhilarating or appallingly untidy. She leaned toward the latter especially after she'd tossed the pitcher of water on him.

He came up spluttering, which was to be expected. Getting doused with water had such an effect on a person. His reaction was likely amplified, however, as he wasn't expecting a pitcher of water to be thrown on him when he entered his carriage, but it couldn't have been helped. She needed him to be coherent when she stated her demands.

"What in God's—" He stopped as he wiped the water from his eyes, blinking into the near darkness of their surroundings. "Lady Alice?" He spoke her name more softly, curiously. And then— "No." He turned to the door, water spraying from his chin as he scrambled to catch hold of the handle, but the carriage was already in motion, and his hasty movements were futile.

"Lord Knighton, you have nothing to fear from me, I promise you."

He gave up on the door and sat back, pressing himself against the opposite bench, arms splayed as if preparing for the rapture. "I think we may have differing viewpoints on that matter, my lady."

"You have my word, my lord. I have no ill intentions. It's only I have a proposition for you, and as an unwed lady, I was forced to take such extreme measures in order to have this conversation with you." She set the empty pitcher aside and folded her hands delicately in her lap as if such a reasonable gesture might calm him. "If society didn't insist on such arcane rules, I wouldn't have resorted to such barbarity."

He raised an eyebrow, his expression not losing its wariness even as he surveyed her with obvious curiosity. "And I suppose the water was necessary as well?"

She glanced at the pitcher on the bench beside her. "I couldn't have known whether or not you were inebriated, and I need your full attention for this conversation. The water was to rouse you to your senses."

"I am not in the least inebriated, Lady Alice, but I'm rather regretting that now."

She flexed her hands together and apart, willing her courage to hold. "I promise to be swift, my lord, and then you may return to your social schedule. I presume you're on your way to a dalliance of some sort?" She could feel the muscles in her hands had begun to twitch, her fingers pulsing with the need to fidget, and she willed herself to hold still.

It had taken sheer bravado to steal into his carriage, and she was quickly learning bravado was an ephemeral creature, prone to flight at a moment's notice. She swallowed and took a measured breath, willing her nerves to calm. She couldn't give up now, and besides, emotion had nothing to do with this encounter. It was merely science which brought her to this man's carriage in the middle of the night, and science was comfortingly cold and analytical.

His expression didn't change at her words, but his eyes searched her face, the hint of curiosity remaining in his gaze. "I don't believe my social schedule is any of your concern, my lady."

His words stung, but he was right. She had no claim on this man. In fact, she'd only met him the week previous at her sister's wedding. It wasn't even as though he were an old friend of the family, which would have served to alleviate the oddness of the situation.

He was only Ransom Shepard, the Earl of Knighton, London's most notorious rogue. A designation that made him perfect for her endeavors.

She straightened her shoulders against the bench at her back, her nerves settling as she remembered the reason she was there.

"You're quite right. I do apologize. I've come to ask for your assistance, my lord."

"I have no intention of marrying any time soon, Lady Alice, so if you believe by trapping me—"

She wrinkled her nose. "Who said anything about marriage?" She couldn't think of a more appalling idea. It was all perfectly well for her sisters to wed, and really, it was most advantageous for them, and Alice wished them all the happiness they might find there. But no, marriage was not for her. It never had been.

Knighton's death grip on the carriage eased, and his hands slipped from the upholstery to fall at his sides. "Isn't that what this is about?"

"Good heavens, no. I have no intention of marrying as well. On that, we are agreed."

His stricken expression dissolved then, his brow furrowing. "Then why on earth are you in my carriage? Tossing water on me no less."

She tilted her head as if she were dealing with an unruly experiment. "I've already explained the water, my lord. As to the other, I should like your assistance with a matter that your reputation would suggest you have a great deal of experience in. As this endeavor is very important to me, I should only like the best in the field."

"And what would this endeavor be?"

"I should like you to seduce me." The words still sounded wooden to her, but as she was so inexperienced in this realm, she didn't know how else to word it.

Knighton watched her, his eyes unmoving for several seconds, and then—

"No." He turned to the door again, his hands scrambling for the handle just as the carriage made a turn, and he was thrown against the door. He shoved himself back on the bench, pushing himself even farther away from her this time, if that were possible.

"My lord, must I point out that we're in a moving conveyance? There is nowhere for you to run. Now I should like your attention on the matter at hand."

"I do not seduce debutantes. I might be a rogue, but I have principles."

She folded her hands more securely in her lap. "That's wonderful then as I am no debutante. You may not realize, but I've never had a season. While I might be out, there is no formality about that matter, so you have no need to worry about my status as a debutante."

"I think your sisters and uncle would disagree with your viewpoint."

This made her pause. "Of course they wouldn't disagree. I've always made my views on the subject very clear. My sisters know—"

"Your sisters know the advantages a married woman has and likely wish the same for you whether you have stated otherwise or not. In that vein, I must insist I return you to your home." He made to rap on the roof of the carriage to get the driver's attention and paused. "Are you required at home or do you have a social obligation you're skirting tonight, Lady Alice?"

She opened her mouth to answer and shook her head. "No, that's not the point of this at all. My lord, I must insist that you consider my request."

"I will not consider your request. I do not dally with debutantes. That's the end of it."

"But you're London's most notorious rogue."

He stilled at this, his eyes narrowing. "That might be, but even a rogue operates by certain standards."

"Are you suggesting that I am somehow beneath you?"

He swallowed then and looked away. "Not right now, and if I have anything to say about that matter, you never will be."

She frowned. "I don't understand."

He shook his head, sitting forward on the bench. "Lady Alice." He spoke her name slowly as if she were a child, and the skin tightened at the back of her neck. "You must trust me to know what is best in this situation. Your reputation—"

"I will trust my own intuition in this matter, my lord, but thank you for your concern. Now then, what will it take for you to accept my proposal?"

He sat back. "You're serious about this."

"Of course I am."

"Why?"

The single word stopped her. She hadn't expected him to ask questions. She had thought her mere presence and the fact she was a willing participant would be enough to get him to accept her proposition. The first lick of misgiving crept over her skin, and she pressed the palms of her hands together, pushing the feeling away.

In her mind, she pictured the letter as she'd held it in her hands, shaking ever so slightly with anticipation. Anticipation that had turned to dismay and heartbreak.

Your curiosity is unnatural.

She swallowed, pushing the memory away to focus on the goal in front of her. The one thing that had the power to banish that letter and its contents from her mind. "As I mentioned, I have no intention of marrying, but as a scientist, I have certain curiosities and questions about the relations between a man and a woman. I should like your assistance in answering my queries."

"You wish to analyze sex?"

She pursed her lips before saying, "Not just the act itself, my lord. I should like to explore all degrees of intimacy between the sexes."

"In the name of science?"

She nodded. She rather enjoyed the idea when he framed it like that. He needn't ever know her true reasons for pursuing him.

Unnatural.

"Yes, precisely. As I will not marry, I have no other way of discovering such things unless I make an arrangement such as this. So you see, you mustn't worry about any kind of entanglement from me, my lord. I wish for our relationship to remain strictly professional."

"Except for the part where you wish for me to seduce you."

"I don't see how that should matter. Emotions have nothing to do with what I wish to attempt."

He leaned back, relaxing for the first time since she'd tossed the water on him. "Darling, I'm afraid that's the first thing you must learn. Seduction is never without emotion."

"Ah, I see where the problem lies. You are confusing emotions with sensation. I should very much wish to explore all the sensations that may be produced in one's seduction. It is the emotions that are unnecessary."

The grin slipped from his lips, and she felt a sudden pang at its loss. "You really believe that." It wasn't a question, and there was something rather forlorn in his tone.

She straightened her shoulders again. "Of course I believe it. I've made a practice of it actually. One can accomplish a great deal more when one separates the emotion out. It's rather a splendid way of doing things."

He watched her for several seconds, and she felt the odd urge to fix her hair.

Finally he sat up. "What's in it for me?"

"I beg your pardon?"

"You're asking me to break one of the few rules I live by, Lady Alice. Surely you didn't expect me to simply agree to this proposal."

The lick of misgiving tripped inside of her, sending her stomach into a sudden somersault as if she'd misjudged a step. If she closed her eyes then, she could picture the letter in its entirety.

Find yourself a husband if you can, although if your submission to this revered scientific journal is any evidence of the matter, perhaps spinsterhood would be a better fit.

She drew a measured breath, willing her heart to calm. "I don't think I understand."

He leaned back and crossed one ankle over the opposite knee, exuding an ease she had never experienced before, and she clenched her hands more tightly in her lap.

"I can have any woman in London." He paused and seemed to rethink his words. "I haven't traveled much outside of Britain, but I would be so bold as to suggest I could have any woman anywhere. Why should I seduce you?"

Her stomach clenched, and she pressed her hands to it trying to quell the sense of misgiving growing inside of her. It wasn't happening. It wasn't. He was only bargaining with her. It was to be expected. She was not going to be rejected. Again. He was not going to prove the letter writer to be right.

"I didn't realize you required a reason beyond the fact that I am a willing female."

He laughed, the sound harsh and unforgiving in the small space. He leaned forward, elbows on his knees, and in the little light there was in the carriage, his eyes flashed blue, and for a moment, her body tightened, responding to his handsomeness, his charm, and then it went still again.

"Lady Alice, I regret to inform you that I do not merely seduce women because I can. I must desire them in some fashion." Those blue eyes assessed her, traveling down to where her booted feet sat firmly on the floor of the carriage and back up to the top of her unadorned felt hat. "And honestly, I do not see anything here to entice me."

The familiar cold of reality swept through her. She wanted to close her eyes, to allow the memories of past rejection to course over her without seeing the one being made in that moment, the one she would add to all the rest. The evidence of her worthlessness.

The letter writer had been correct.

She couldn't close her eyes though. She couldn't look away. Because a very small part of her, a part of her she had long tried to deny, wanted to see his blue eyes. Wanted to memorize the way they looked in that moment. The way he leaned toward her, his chiseled jaw so determined, his firm lips curved into a grin. It was all at her expense, but it needn't matter. She'd never been this close to a man before, and she likely would never be again, and she wanted to remember it no matter how awful it was.

This was the man who desired every woman in London.

Every woman except her.

She gathered the pitcher and rapped once on the ceiling of the carriage. "I'm sorry to have wasted your time," she said.

She alighted before he could say anything else, the pitcher held firmly to her chest as if it could stop her from shattering. She need only walk, and soon she'd forget the encounter entirely, and the unfeeling coldness that kept her safe would be repaired. All would be well then. She had been foolish to think her scheme would work anyway. To think, someone like the Earl of Knighton should wish to seduce her? What had she been thinking?

She had been thinking what she always thought. Maybe this time things would be different.

Her boots rang out on the pavement as she let the night fog swallow her whole.

* * *

WHERE THE BLOODY hell did she think she was going?

They may have been in Mayfair, but it was still the middle of the night. She would be an easy and welcomed target for any footpad lying in wait. He reached for the door and cursed himself for his hesitation in following her, but her words had rattled him.

She wanted him to seduce her. He had heard similar requests from more women than he could remember in the past ten years, but he'd never heard them spoken with such sterile exactness.

She wished to be seduced, but she thought to go about it without emotions getting involved.

Why?

He cursed himself again. He shouldn't care why. He shouldn't care about her at all, and yet there he was, the need to go after her seizing his body like a fever. He didn't dally with debutantes on principle. Except his reasons for such a rule were likely not what she would have thought. He avoided debutantes not for the potential danger they carried, namely social-climbing mothers and money-hungry fathers.

The reason he avoided them was that debutantes were more likely to still believe in love.

Even being that close to the idea of love was enough to have his stomach seizing and the acrid taste of memories fill his mouth. He'd rather risk getting caught by an irate husband with a brace of pistols than get trapped in a conversation about love with a naive, young lady.

He pushed through the door of his carriage and dropped to the ground, the sound of his boots hitting pavement loud in the quiet of the night around him. They were in the thick of Mayfair, and the facades of London's noble homes peered down on him like leering ghouls in the dark. He signaled to his driver to wait and struck off in the direction he had seen her go, but uneasiness crept over him. She must have been walking quickly because she had already disappeared from the street they had stopped on. He called back to his driver to stay where the carriage had stopped as he sped up, taking the first corner he came to.

He spotted her immediately as she passed beneath a streetlamp two doors ahead of him down the street. Relief swept through him. He may not have wished to be discovered alone with her, and he certainly did not wish to get entangled in whatever scheme she plotted, but there was something about Lady Alice that made him wish to protect her.

It was a ridiculous and unfamiliar feeling, and he tried to push it aside, but he knew somehow it would not be dismissed. Perhaps it was because she was now the sister-in-law to his dearest and oldest friend, Ashfield Riggs, the

Marquess of Aylesford. Whatever it was, he had to see her safely home, and then he could put this whole night behind him.

He reached for her arm, but his hand never made contact as she spun about, the pitcher raised in a threatening arc. Deftly, he swung out his hand and blocked her trajectory, but her other hand was already coming up, reaching for the reticule that swung from the opposite wrist. He wondered briefly what was in her reticule that she had tried to grab before her eyes lit with comprehension.

"Do you not know it is unwise to sneak up on a lady in the middle of the night? You can never tell of what she might be capable." Lady Alice's lips pursed, an expression he was coming to find was common for her and one which was riddled with nuance. Was she annoyed? Frustrated? Displeased?

"Do you always assault gentlemen with water pitchers?"

"Only when it is deserved," she said, shaking her arm loose and lowering the pitcher. "Otherwise I simply use my knife."

He took an involuntary step back, his eyes going to her reticule. "You're armed?"

She tugged at the sleeves of her dress, and he realized she wore no shawl. The hour grew late, and he worried suddenly that she might be cold. What a ludicrous thought. The woman had just tried to maim him, and he was concerned for her comfort.

"Of course I am, Lord Knighton. Do you take me for a fool? This may be Mayfair, but it only means we're more valuable targets, wouldn't you say?"

He looked about them, remembering where they were. He took her arm, but she immediately tugged it free, her head tilting to eye him as though he were a venomous snake.

"I beg your pardon."

"I will not leave you here alone. We must return to the carriage, and I will have my driver—"

She looked down at the pavement, completely ignoring him.

Stupidly, he followed her gaze. After several seconds of silence, he finally asked, "What is it?"

"I was just confirming that I still have two working feet." She looked up, her lips firm. "You made it sound as though I had lost independent mobility."

It was his turn to firm his lips. He took a moment to swallow and draw a deep breath. "Lady Alice," he began.

And she turned and walked away from him. He blinked, once more hesitating to follow her as she so deftly rattled him.

"Lady Alice." He spoke her name more firmly now, tension coursing through his muscles, another unfamiliar sensation. What was this woman doing to him? He took two steps toward her and stopped. This was asinine. She was clearly finished with him, and he should leave her be. After all, she'd already proven she could take care of herself.

He watched her for a second longer and then turned about, prepared to head back to his carriage and never see the woman again.

Except he was stopped when a man emerged from the shadows, the glint of a knife in his hands clearly visible in the dark.

Mother of God, was there no end to this farce?

He clenched his fists and forced them to relax. He had no wish for violence that night, and he really wished he hadn't left the carriage.

"Empty yer pockets, guv," the man said in a tone that whistled through his missing front teeth. "The lady's right, I'm afraid. Yer just worth more to me than most."

Slowly, Ransom slid one foot beside the other. Keeping a

careful distance, he turned them about, his arms raised innocently.

"I have no desire for trouble, my good man," he said, keeping his voice low and steady. If he could get the man on the opposite side, he had a chance to run for the carriage, and then he would have no need to pummel the life from this stranger. "I was merely passing through."

He was nearly completely turned around when the man made a swipe with his knife. The blade cut through the air directly in front of his torso, and he swore he could feel the deadly metal catch on the fabric of his coat. He lurched backward, startling the footpad, and the man lunged with his knife.

Ransom deftly caught the man's wrist, twisting it neatly until the blade fell helplessly from the footpad's fingers, but it needn't have mattered.

The crack of porcelain against skull rang through the night, and the man dropped to the ground with a muffled thud, falling neatly beside his useless knife.

"Must I walk *you* home, my lord? I shouldn't wish for any further trouble to befall you."

He looked to find Lady Alice standing on the other side of the prone man, her arms akimbo as though she were a governess scolding a recalcitrant child. He wondered if the suggested image was so strong because of her plain dress, the way her features were pinched by how tightly she wore her hair, or if it was those ridiculous spectacles. Combined it brought back startlingly clear memories of his own tutors.

She must have seen something in her perusal of him because her arms suddenly dropped, and she stepped over the poor man she had just bludgeoned as if he weren't there at all. She stopped in front of him, dangerously close, and reached out as if to touch him. He should have stopped her, but instead, he stood transfixed, watching her solitary finger poke him in the chest. No, not poke him. She was fiddling with his jacket.

"He got you." Her eyes flashed to him, and he was startled by the real concern in her gaze. "Are you injured? Do you require medical assistance? I'm well versed on subjects of anatomy and would be happy to offer aid."

For a split second, he pictured her hands on his body. All over his body. Those long, slender fingers trailing their way down his back, across his hips and around to his stomach, dipping farther—

He stepped back so quickly he tripped on the pavement. She snatched at him, seizing his lapels until she ratcheted him back against her chest. He froze, unable to even blink, as he stood with his arms straight out from his sides. He could not touch her. No matter what, he couldn't lay a single finger on her.

She was hiding an extraordinary bosom under that plain gown. He felt every detail of it as she pressed herself against his chest.

"Heavens, have you lost a lot of blood then? Are you feeling faint?" She had raised her voice, practically shouting at him as if he swayed on the edge of consciousness and might be hard of hearing. "I must examine the wound." Her fingers went to the buttons of his waistcoat.

His senses snapped back into place, ringing echoing in his ears as if his mind were rattling through this terrible reality he had stumbled into. He pried her fingers loose and took another, albeit far more careful, step away from her.

"Lady Alice," he finally managed. "I am quite well. I assure you. The knife only caught the lapel of my jacket. I am uninjured."

A line between her brow suggested she did not believe him. "I still think I should—" That damnable hand reached for him again, and he swatted it away, stepping back yet again.

"Lady Alice." He eyed her sternly, but she continued to study the place on his jacket where the fiend's knife had sliced the fabric.

"I have not forgotten my name, my lord. You mustn't keep repeating it." She followed him in his befuddled attempt at escape, but her sedate walk was far more graceful than his stumbling retreat. "You must let me examine you. Wounds if left untreated can fester, and we wouldn't wish for you—"

They'd reached the corner, and he glanced to his right. His carriage was only a few feet away now. But if he brought her back to the carriage, he would be trapped inside with her. How had his evening spun so terribly out of his control?

His hands shot out and grabbed her shoulders before he realized his intent, and he tugged her forward. Shock made her pliable in his arms and without hesitation, he bent his head, blessedly silencing her with a kiss.

For the first time, he realized how quiet it was around them. There were no grand balls in that section of Mayfair that night, and the streets were silent. The fog had started to thicken, and he wondered how late the hour grew. He was dimly aware of these thoughts as though they were separate from himself. There but not there.

Because the only thing he was aware of then was Alice. The feel of her under his hands, the taste of her against his lips, the sound of her gasp as he tilted his head, deepened the kiss. Belatedly he realized it must have been her first kiss as she froze, unmoving beneath his hands. Still, he didn't stop. This was what she wanted, and he was giving it to her. He let the kiss linger for a few seconds longer, taking it far enough to satisfy but not so far as to be perilous.

Then he stepped back and before she could open her eyes, he took her hand and led her the few stumbling steps to the carriage door. He placed her inside the conveyance and shut the door before she had fully roused. He called up to his driver to take her home. The man nodded once and sent the vehicle into motion.

It must have startled Lady Alice from her stupor because her face appeared at the window, her alert features pressed to the glass. He watched her as the carriage rumbled away and thought about how he had lied to her.

He found Alice Atwood entirely too enticing, which meant he must stay away from her at all costs.

CHAPTER 2

*S*he stumbled through the front door, catching herself on the table that sat in the foyer with an ungraceful crash. Uncle Herman popped into the foyer from the drawing room off the main corridor, his sparse gray hair unusually billowy in the early morning hours.

"Alice, love, what's happened?" His eyes were huge behind the smudged lenses of his spectacles, and he held a copy of *Conversations in Chemistry* by Marcus Dillmore FRS open in his hands, his fingers curling tensely into the fresh leather cover of the book.

She gave a wave of her hand in the direction of the door. "The latch stuck again, I'm afraid." Given how turbulent her thoughts and emotions were, she was surprised at how even her voice was as she gave the lie.

Ransom Shepard, the Earl of Knighton, had kissed her.

He had refused her and *then* he had kissed her. How confusing. This was precisely why she preferred science. There were inputs and outcomes, and nothing so chaotic as human interaction.

But wasn't that exactly why she had approached him in the first place?

If anyone were to give her insight into the matter it would be London's greatest rogue.

But he had said no.

There was a single lamp still lit on the table beside her, and it cast wild shadows about the entrance. Uncle Herman appeared particularly rumpled standing there with the book like a shield before him.

"I do hope you weren't waiting up for me." She tried to make out the face of the grandfather clock opposite, but the light was too dim. How long had she been out?

With Adaline and Amelia married and only Uncle Herman left in the Biggleswade house, it was rather easy to come and go as she pleased, but it was upsetting to think she may have kept her gentle uncle from his bed.

It was Uncle Herman's turn to wave a hand as though brushing off her concerns. "I had no such intention, but then I don't exactly know the time. Is the hour late?" He looked down as if just realizing he held a book in his hands, and even in the dim lantern light, she saw the color spring to his cheeks. "I suppose I got rather carried away with Dillmore's new work."

She really couldn't fault her uncle for that. Dillmore's work in crystallization could be rather consuming. She shed her hat and gloves before propelling her uncle in the direction of the stairs.

"As compelling as Dillmore's work may be, I'm afraid it is rather late, and you should be in bed."

Uncle Herman's eyebrows shot up behind his spectacles. She wondered sometimes if he had more hair there than on his head. It was an interesting and complex hypothesis, and she was sometimes forced to make herself look away lest she get caught up in deciphering the volume of hair above his eyes versus that which lingered over the tops of his ears.

"Is it then? Well, I suppose I could turn in." His hands drooped as if he suddenly realized exactly how spent he was. But then he stopped suddenly at the bottom of the stairs, his gaze flying to hers. "If the hour is late, what were you doing out?"

Uncle Herman had only come to live with the Atwood sisters when their father was lost at sea in his last attempt at securing a new fortune to save the Biggleswade title. She had never known her uncle before then aside from the infrequent unflattering mentions made by her father and mother. Poor Uncle Herman had been made the new Earl of Biggleswade upon her father's death, and she still wasn't sure who was more surprised by this, Alice and her sisters or Uncle Herman himself. Regardless, the man had come to be a beloved member of their small family even if Amelia and Adaline had married and left the Biggleswade home so soon after his arrival.

She threaded her arm through his as she pulled him toward the stairs again. "Oh, it was nothing so interesting. Simply an experiment gone awry. I'm afraid I'm as guilty as you in that matter. I let my studies get the best of me, and I lost track of time." She forced an indelicate yawn as though to suggest the entire matter was of little interest, but Uncle Herman's gaze remained sharp as they climbed the stairs.

"A scientific matter, is it? Well, how did it go awry?"

She paused on the landing, sliding a glance in her uncle's direction. Alice had never been one to confide in another. She had learned early on that it was safest not to, but standing there on the landing with Uncle Herman in the quiet of the night, she wondered if the man could act as a repository for her thoughts, muddled though they were. Perhaps if she told him the structure of her problem, he may be able to aid her in its unraveling. She mustn't tell him details. Details were dangerous. But she could disguise her scheme in more scholarly terms.

Without mention of the letter, of course.

"Well, it's a rather simple experiment. One of cause and effect, and I'm afraid when I applied the catalyst the material did not respond as I hypothesized."

Uncle Herman's eyebrows came together. "Interesting. Was the material organic, mineral, or…" He let his voice trail off as they gained the upper floor.

"Organic."

He scratched his chin. "What are its primary elements?"

She studied the carpet at her feet. "Er, carbon, hydrogen, oxygen."

"And what was the catalyst?"

She had asked the Earl of Knighton to seduce her. She couldn't very well say that to Uncle Herman.

"The application of force," she said instead.

Uncle Herman stopped again, his hand curled around the banister that ran the length of the upper floor's gallery while the other hand held Dillmore's book absently to his chest. His gaze was directed at the ceiling, but she knew he was not studying the intricacies of the plaster medallions that dotted its surface.

"So an application of force was made on an organic material, and the expected response was?"

"Movement."

"And what was the actual outcome?"

"Resistance."

"Ah," Uncle Herman breathed, twirling one end of his mustache between his thumb and forefinger. "Friction. A nuisance if you ask me." He dropped his hand and turned to meet her gaze. "Have you tried applying a measure of lubricant of some kind or will it contaminate the experiment protocol?"

For a moment, she forgot this was a made-up experiment. It was an interesting proposal, and she wondered how lubricant would affect the veracity of a force experiment. She shook her head. This was not at all the point.

"No, I did not apply lubricant. I hadn't expected to need it."

Knighton didn't desire her. She hadn't expected passion or lust from him. It was only her own response that interested her. A response she was hoping would prove the letter writer wrong. But her assumption that a rogue would bed any female had been inaccurate. She wasn't even desirable enough for a man who made it a practice to bed every available female.

She should have known better. She had thought the sexual act could be done without the bother of emotion, but it might have been that Knighton required some level of... lubricant. But she had nothing to offer. That had been a lesson she had learned all too early in her life.

"I see," Uncle Herman muttered now. "So the organic matter should have created the desired result with the application of force and yet failed to do so?"

"Yes." She rubbed the toe of her boot against the carpet. "I suppose the force being applied was not adequate." She shook her head. "Perhaps the force was adequate but not of the right substance."

"Tell me something. What is it that is of most importance in this experiment? Is it the application of force? Is it the organic material? Or is it the end result?"

Her stomach tightened. She hadn't thought of what she was attempting to do in such analytical terms such as this, and suddenly the entire scheme broke apart in her mind, and she could arrange its various pieces like she often did with mathematical problems.

"I suppose it's the end result. There's a desired outcome that I am seeking."

Unnatural.

The word played over and over again in her head, daring her to eradicate it.

Uncle Herman straightened away from the banister with a blustering sound of affirmation. "Well then, it would seem you must change one of the two variables. Either the force being applied or the organic material upon which the force acts."

Uncle Herman drifted down the hall, but she forgot to follow. Her mind sorted through what he had just said. If she were the force and Knighton was the organic material she had plied with her offer, then of those two variables there was only one she could change.

"Alice?"

She blinked. Uncle Herman had traveled several feet down the corridor and picked up a lamp left on the table in the hallway where the family's rooms started.

"I think you're right, Uncle Herman," she said, moving to catch up with him. "The other variables in the equation would need to change in order to affect the outcome. It's all very simple."

How had she not seen it?

Because Knighton's rejection of her had been devastating, made so much worse by its unexpectedness. It had been consuming and ending because it had been a familiar occurrence in her life. From the moment she was born a girl, she had been rejected. What was once more?

Only why had it hurt quite so much coming from Knighton? She hadn't known the man for very long, and he did not have the kind of academic reputation that would earn her respect.

But he had kissed her. And she'd never been kissed before.

Absently she touched her fingers to her lips, the echo of his kiss still haunting her.

"Precisely," Uncle Herman said with another of his blustery affirmation noises. "Now you must only determine if the force can be changed or if the organic matter must."

She met her uncle's gaze, her hand dropping to her side. "Thank you, Uncle. I'm rather glad Dillmore's findings kept you awake. I would have been vexed by this problem all night without your assistance."

Uncle Herman laughed. "I shouldn't think so, dear. You would have reached the same conclusion eventually." He opened the door to his rooms and bade her good night.

The corridor grew dark after he closed his door, the only lit lamp still in his hand and likely forgotten. It needn't matter. She had traversed the corridors of Biggleswade House in the dark numerous times beginning as a child when she would sneak down to the library long after Nurse had put them all to bed.

She entered her rooms and found a lamp burning on the rosewood table she used for a desk. It startled her finding it there. It was only recently that the Biggleswade title had had enough funds to employ adequate staff that would have been responsible for such a thoughtful gesture. She swallowed, knowing the funds had come at an exorbitant cost, Amelia's marriage to a reclusive duke known as the Ghoul of Greyfair. She forced her shoulders down as she recalled how happy her sister found herself married to said duke, and all had ended better than expected.

Alice made quick work of pulling the pins from her hair and letting the long, straight, dark locks fall down her back.

She massaged her tired scalp for a few blissful seconds, letting a moan of pleasure escape her lips. She was only grateful she wasn't forced to twist her thick hair into the convoluted constructs debutantes aspired to this season.

Within seconds she was at her desk, unlacing her boots at the same time she tried to pull a clean sheet of paper from the drawer of her desk. She pushed aside books on botany and geology and the pamphlet on the opening of the new observatory at College Park she had picked up at the library last week and set the clean sheet of paper directly in the middle of her desk.

She paused, her fingers still twined with the laces of her boots. There was nothing quite so satisfying as a blank piece of paper. She finished with her footwear and picked up her quill.

If the variable of force, herself, could not be changed in the equation as it was she who wished to be seduced, then the only other possibility was changing the organic matter. Er, Knighton.

The problem was quite simple. She needed another rogue.

Dipping her quill in a fresh pot of ink, she scratched out a list of all of London's most well-known rogues. Somewhere in that list she would find the right organic material for her experiment.

* * *

Why did she carry a knife?

Did she know how to use it?

And why, three days after his late-night encounter with her, was he still thinking about Lady Alice Atwood?

He snatched a glass of champagne from a passing waiter just to have something to do with his hands. He vibrated

24

with an impatience unfamiliar to him as his thoughts tumbled one over the other, and the glass of champagne was a welcomed distraction even if the stuff was watered down and flat. The Earl of Sylvan was not known for extravagance, and that apparently extended to how he treated his guests.

Lady Felix had not been pleased he'd missed their meeting the night Alice had abducted him. He wasn't surprised by that, and he felt a note of caution. He couldn't let it happen again. He had spent the past ten years carefully crafting the reputation he desired, and he couldn't let some ambitious debutante get the better of him.

It was as though he were consumed by thoughts of only Lady Alice, and such a state gave him a great deal of unease. He wasn't used to caring about others. There were few members of his family left for whom he cared and a smattering of true friends, Ash, Lady Alice's newest brother-in-law, being one of them, but this pulse inside of him when his mind turned to Lady Alice was far deeper than mere care.

In a flash, he was back to that night. It was as if his heart beat anew, pulsing a staccato in his chest. He willed the memory away. It was only the unusual circumstances that had caused such a reaction. Nothing more.

But he couldn't deny the unfamiliar need to protect her. Perhaps that was nothing more than association. She was related in marriage to his best friend after all. He was only being a gentleman if he looked out for her. He mustn't worry over any deeper emotions.

In general, he avoided feelings toward others. It was far safer that way. The only emotions he wanted to experience were the ones directed *at* him. The ones he had once believed could fill the abyss that had been left in the middle of his soul the day his mother left, the one he had never been able to repair.

The yawning blackness that had crept over him until it

seemed to be all he could feel had receded in recent days. That happened from time to time but usually only when he was considering a horse to add to his stables at The Falls or an issue raised by his tenants. But this distraction was something else entirely.

She wasn't even pretty. Well, actually, he couldn't tell if she was pretty. It was another thing about her that confused him. Her dresses were plain, if not drab, her hair was always wound too tightly, low against the nape of her neck, and those damned spectacles. He wondered for a fleeting moment if she was *trying* to look plain. He stopped with the glass of champagne at his lips. Why would a woman do such a thing?

He discarded the unfinished glass with the next footman who walked by and dove into the throng at the edge of the ballroom. Lady Mallory, the wife of a cold, demanding earl, had suggested Ransom request a dance from her this evening, and he wondered if she had arrived. It would do him no good to stand at the fringes, ruminating about a woman who would cause him nothing but trouble when a perfectly acceptable lady had made an overture toward him.

He was halfway across the room when he realized he was trying to picture Lady Alice without her spectacles. He shook his head and blinked several times, drawing more than one curious look in his direction. He had to stop this.

It was, of course, at that moment he spotted her.

At first, he thought he was seeing things, an illusion conjured by his rampaging thoughts. But then he realized she was actually there, standing not more than a couple of yards from him. He couldn't understand what she was doing there. She had said herself she wasn't a debutante. She'd had no season. But—

She was speaking to Amory Jenkins, Viscount Crandall.

He froze, the crowd about him jostling as he stopped his progression so suddenly.

If there were a more notorious rogue than Ransom himself, it was Lord Crandall.

Icy terror shot through him, followed swiftly by the urgent need to get to her, to—God, save her.

Their conversation from that night in the carriage came roaring back to him. She wished to be seduced. No, more than that. She wanted to learn every detail about seduction. She had thought—

His feet were moving before he could finish his thought, but Lady Felix stepped in front of him.

"Lord Knighton, a word."

Once more he found himself blinking as he tried to match what was before him with what he had been pursuing. "Lady Felix, I beg your pardon. I haven't the time at the moment."

Lady Felix was a good deal older than he, but her face was still unlined. Her thin lips firmed as her stare turned to a glare.

"Ransom, if you think I'm going to—"

"Really very sorry. I must be off." He pushed past her, but he didn't miss her gasp of shock as he did so. Word of the slight would spread quickly, and he couldn't fathom the damage it would do to his reputation. The reputation he had worked so hard to cultivate, the one thing that mattered to him, the one thing that kept him safe.

He didn't think of any of that though because when he pushed through the last of the crowd, Lady Alice was gone.

So was Lord Crandall.

Later he would think about how his heart lurched into a gallop, how his hands shook, how he frantically searched the crowd for some sign of either of them. Why did Lady Alice have this effect on him? More importantly, how could he stop it?

He wasn't thinking though, not clearly enough anyway, as he once more surged through the crowd. Seconds later he broke free of the throng around the refreshment table and found himself in a quiet alcove. An empty, quiet alcove. He flexed his fingers into fists and forced them to relax again as he turned about to look at the crowd once more. But as he turned, he caught sight of a shadow in the recesses of the alcove.

A door. A small door hidden at the very back of the space.

He plunged ahead, not thinking if someone should see him or caring what it might mean if he emerged later with Lady Alice. He had to find her. Lord Crandall was not the sort with whom she should be associating. The man was a rogue. Well, Ransom was considered a rogue as well, but Crandall was despicable. He held no qualms about deflowering a debutante. If the rumors were true, Lord Crandall held no qualms about much.

He stopped, shaken both by his thoughts and where he found himself. The door in the alcove lead to a small, dim corridor lit only by the sporadic sconce along the wall. It was hardly inviting and rather obvious guests were not permitted here, and yet the trail of closed doors stampeding down the length of it suggested ample opportunities for a clandestine rendezvous.

Between a debutante and the man willing to deflower her.

He marched down the corridor, throwing open each door as he came to it. Each time he was met with a silent dark room. He paused long enough to make certain the room was truly empty before moving on. It wasn't until he'd thrown open the fourth door that a voice behind him startled him.

"What on earth are you doing?"

His hand flexed on the doorknob as he turned to take in

Lady Alice, standing as she usually did, arms akimbo, her frown fierce. But she was alone. His eyes swept up and down the corridor to make certain, but Lord Crandall was nowhere in sight.

"I could ask you the same thing," he said before he grabbed her and dragged her through the door he had just opened.

He clearly had not thought this through. This room was far darker than the others he had been in, and it soon became clear it might not have been a room at all. He had only just barely shut the door behind them, sealing out what little light there had been when he collided with a wall. He fell backward and into Lady Alice who sucked in a sharp breath at the collision. She shoved him back, sending him into the wall again.

"What is the matter with you? Keep off of me."

He bounced against the wall and came against her once more, but this time she squirmed against him. He tried to pull his hands free so he could catch her shoulders and stop her from squirming, but she continued to push at him. Except there was nowhere for him to go.

"Lady Alice, you must cease. There isn't room—" He got one arm free but not before he collided with something soft and round. Oh God, was that her breast? Would she notice if he tried to snatch another feel? Jesus, he was worse than Crandall.

"Lord Knighton, you made it perfectly clear you have no desire to—"

It was his turn to suck in a breath as her elbow jabbed his stomach. Finally his second arm came free, and he found her shoulders in the dark, pinning her to the wall he had bounced off of not moments before.

"Lady Alice, stop. We seem to be in a cupboard, and if you continue in your attempts to get away from me, you will only make this situation worse." She stilled so completely beneath his hands, he wondered if he had frightened her. "I'm going to remove my hands now. Please do not try to move. There isn't the space for it."

He couldn't see her clearly in the dark. She was a mere outline against the darker black of the wall behind her. But he slowly raised his hands, and she didn't make a single motion. He wasn't even sure if she was breathing.

"Lord Knighton." The words were sharp and brittle with accusation, and he made the mistake of holding up a hand to cut her off. Said hand struck her breast again—at least, he believed it was her breast—and he closed his eyes in frustration.

"Please, just Ransom. This cupboard is too small for titles."

There was a pause, and the next she spoke her voice was strangely tentative. "Ransom. I should like to know what you're about."

"I should ask you the same thing."

There was a rustling, and her elbow found his stomach again, and he thought she might have tried to put her hands to her hips. He wondered if she always stood with such dominance, and he found he rather liked the idea. Blast it.

"I was not the one to suggest we have this conversation in a cupboard. I return the question to you."

"What are you doing with Lord Crandall?" Dear God, was that jealousy in his voice? Certainly not. He had no claims on Lady Alice, and he certainly had no right—

But he had felt protective of her, hadn't he?

His stomach twisted at the danger he saw lurking in these new and unfamiliar emotions she caused in him.

"That's none of your concern."

"You're going to ask him to seduce you, aren't you?"

Her lips parted, a soft, stunned breath escaping. It was

only a flutter of movement that he could make out in the dark, but he suddenly wanted to kiss the surprise from her mouth.

"How do you know that?"

"He's the obvious choice. There isn't a more deplorable rogue in London."

"You find him deplorable?"

"Of course he's deplorable. He has no rules about virgins."

She shifted, and he sensed she had tilted her head in the darkness. They were so close, he could sense the ghost of her breath, the quiet rise and fall of her chest, and for a brief moment, he recalled the soft plumpness of her breast. He had been surprised by its fullness, but it only added fuel to the evidence he had discovered that night when she'd been pressed against him. He wondered once again what she was hiding behind that drab exterior.

"Rules about virgins? Is there some sort of code of honor amongst rogues that I am unaware of?"

He frowned. "That's hardly the point. Stay away from Crandall."

"You're telling me what to do?" He could almost imagine the look of shock that painted her features if the icy pitch of her voice were any clue.

"Lady Alice, you do not—"

"It's Alice, and do not begin to tell me what I do and do not want. I'm perfectly capable of determining my own desires, and I wish to be seduced." She planted both hands against his chest then as if she planned to push him away, and the heat of her touch scorched him.

"You are going to proceed with your plan?" His brain melted at the thought, his need for self-preservation warring with the much stronger instinct to protect her.

"Of course I am. I can hardly discover what I wish to learn if I simply give up because you declined to engage in my endeavor." She pushed at him. "Now if you'll excuse me, Lord Crandall is waiting for me—"

"I'll do it." The words were out before he could stop them, and he worried his heart would rip from his chest at the sudden trepidation that spilled through him.

Her hands relaxed against his chest, her fingers no longer pushing. He'd surprised her, again, and he hated how much he waited for her response. He focused on her touch, the sound of her breath, anything to stop himself from examining why he was suddenly so tense, why a fear he had thought long banished and forgotten was suddenly emerging once again inside of him.

"But you said no."

"Of course I said no. I have some respect regardless of what my reputation would suggest, but I will not let Crandall touch you."

Her head went back, and he heard the rustle of her hair against the wall.

"You won't let Crandall touch me?" Her voice was soft and had it been anyone else, he might have called it wondering, but Alice was far too pragmatic for such fanciful notions. "Why? You don't even like me."

"Who said I don't like you?"

He felt more than saw her frown. "You've made your feelings toward me perfectly obvious."

"What are you talking about? Besides the other night, we've hardly been in each other's presence and especially not alone. How could you possibly know how I feel about you?" He wished he could see her face. He needed to know what feelings played across her features, but then she was likely too controlled to allow such a weakness.

She hesitated, and he wasn't sure how, but he suddenly sensed she was about to lie to him.

"Perhaps I was mistaken. I beg your pardon. Now if you'll

excuse me, I wish to return to the ball." She made to move around him, which was impossible in the small cupboard without him shifting to allow her to do so, and so, he simply planted his feet and leaned forward, putting his hands on the wall on either side of her head to box her in.

"Do you really wish to leave? I thought you wanted to be seduced." He leaned closer with each word until his lips brushed her ear. He felt her breath stumble and then even out into careful measured breaths. He wasn't sure when it happened, but he suddenly realized if he were to keep Alice safe, he had to give her what she wanted. Even if it meant danger for him. "Do you want me to seduce you, Alice?"

Her lips parted. He felt it against his cheek, but she made no sound. He brushed his lips over her ear, not quite touching her and yet touching her enough to feel her shiver against him.

"Alice?"

"Yes." The word came out as two syllables, and he smiled against the tender spot below her ear.

"Good." He backed away as far as the cupboard would allow him, leaving her slumped against the back wall. "I'm glad we're in agreement. Now you have no need to find Crandall. Shall I escort you back to the ballroom?"

It was a horrible thing to do, toying with her emotions like that, but she'd given him no choice.

She was quiet for a calculating moment, and then she straightened, her silhouette growing rigid in the dark. "I have no need for your escort, my lord." This time when she shoved him, he let her, sliding out of the way to give her access to the door.

She slipped out and went so far as to shut the door behind her, leaving him alone in the dark in a cupboard wondering what the hell he had just gotten himself into.

CHAPTER 3

*F*our hundred thirty-five not four hundred fifty-three.

She scribbled out her mistake with such force she tore the page. She dropped her head into her hands and groaned as she spiked her fingers through the hair at her temples, loosening the tight chignon in grateful relief.

She had been transposing her numbers all morning.

There was no reason for her mind to be this unfocused. The encounter with Ransom the previous night had not been expected, but then, the outcome had been what she'd wished. He had agreed to help her.

So why had he suddenly changed his mind?

Such vacillating behavior was familiar to her, and it was likely this that had her so distracted this morning. She had been the victim of the same pattern of behavior before, and seeing the pattern repeated, she was wary. Her mother would sometimes suddenly take an interest in Alice, and this interest would often lead to a shopping excursion, one in which her mother had claimed to want Alice's input on some book purchases. In truth, it was an excuse to get Alice to another modiste appointment. Her mother had tried several, giving each seamstress the clear instruction to make Alice look less like…well, Alice.

It had been her mother's greatest ambition to mold Alice into something passable and not the coltish young woman Alice had been, her nose stuck in a book and her mind whirling through mathematical equations. But her mother had always been disappointed, and Alice had always been tricked. Every time. Because every time she hoped her mother had truly wished to be with her, had truly cared about the things Alice enjoyed.

She leaned back in her chair and tipped her head to one side, stretching her sore neck muscles. She'd commandeered the large table in the study that morning to have more room for her books, and she'd been at her task for some hours.

Uncle Herman had left just after dawn for a meandering walk through the park to sort through some research that was troubling him, and as he was out of the house for likely most of the day, she had taken liberties with the earl's study. It was easier to lay out the many books she wished to reference in her notes than to be forced to stack them all together on her small rosewood table in her room.

Uncle Herman had passed along this month's news sheet from the Scientific Scholar Society about the possible discovery of a new comet. She was quite certain the identified comet had actually been seen before, and she was now combing through her various astronomy texts to see if she could pinpoint its exact mention.

Not that it would do any good. She had it in writing how the Scientific Scholar Society felt about female academics. Her only wish was that the letter had been signed with a person's name instead of the vague *On behalf of the Scientific Scholar Society* she had found at the bottom of the rejection. It would have been so much easier to pin her frustration onto a single person.

Your curiosity is unnatural.

Unnatural.

The word was like a pendulum, swinging back and forth relentlessly in her mind. She closed her eyes against it and tried to quiet her mind to the task at hand. Even though her endeavor was for her own interests as the Society would never take her findings seriously, she couldn't help but feel the gnawing suspicion that had plagued her since receiving the Society's scathing rejection of her submission to their quarterly journal.

She worried her studies were at an end.

It was this worry coupled with the letter writer's biting pronouncement about her person that had driven her to her rather daring scheme. She knew the danger she was playing with, but she couldn't help it. Something must be done.

All she had ever had was her studies, and if there was nowhere more to go from here, what had she?

Unbidden, she remembered the feel of Ransom's body pressed against her, and suddenly the danger became palatable. She sat up, shaking her head and curling her toes into the carpet. She'd shed her slippers long ago as the feel of the floor beneath her feet was grounding when attempting her studies, and it worked to straighten her wayward thoughts.

She had undertaken this endeavor to gather proof of the letter writer's inaccurate judgment of her. There was nothing unnatural about Alice. Ransom was going to help her prove it.

She sat up at the sound of footsteps in the corridor. The clock on the mantel showed half eleven, certainly too early for Uncle Herman to have returned. When the housekeeper, Mrs. Marble, stepped inside the study seconds later, Alice couldn't stop her eyebrows from going up.

It was only recently they had been able to afford a house-keeper again, and Alice was still growing used to the woman's quiet and efficient ways. Alice smiled in greeting only to have the expression falter at the sight of the silver tray in the woman's hands.

"My lady, there is a gentleman to see you."

Alice didn't have callers. Amelia hadn't had callers, and Adaline had had Ash. She rose and went to Mrs. Marble, peering down at the card on the tray only to blink as though her eyesight were suddenly failing her.

The words *Ransom Shepard, Earl of Knighton*, marched across the hatched pearl white card stock in bold black lettering.

"Show him in, please," she said, keeping her voice remarkably even.

Ransom.

What was he doing here? Was he calling to tell her he'd been mistaken? That he wouldn't engage in her scheme?

Mrs. Marble gave a nod and said, "Yes, of course, ma'am," and left the room.

Alice retreated behind the table holding her books, her hands caressing the back of her abandoned chair as though it could provide some kind of assurance. God, the man had rattled her so much in the few times they had been alone together and now he was here. In daylight. In her home. And—

"Alice."

It wasn't until she heard her name spoken in his deep, even voice that she realized she wasn't wearing her glasses. Or her shoes. She often took off her spectacles when she was alone, and now she scrambled to find where she had discarded them amongst her papers and books even as she retrieved her slippers from under the table. She spotted her spectacles under a treatise on the accessibility of astronomical study just as she slipped on her second slipper, and in her haste to get her spectacles at the same time toppled the book they were hiding under to the floor as she tried to get the spectacles onto her nose.

She made to turn to greet her—well, gentleman caller sounded altogether too strange, though that was what he was —but she collided with an outstretched arm. She squeaked— squeaked?—and jumped backward, slamming into the table at her back.

Ransom's smile was soft and charming, but she couldn't help thinking he was trying to stop a laugh.

"Alice," he said again, his smile deepening. "I didn't mean to startle you." He gestured toward the fallen book. "Allow me."

He finished bending toward the book and snatched it up, placing it carefully on the table.

She sucked in a breath, realizing suddenly that he held a bouquet of flowers in one hand.

Roses. Yellow roses.

No one had ever brought her flowers. Were they, indeed, for her?

A feeling welled up within her, a feeling so foreign she couldn't even name it. It was warm, soft, and whole, but right behind it came the hard edge of wariness. She curled her fingers around the tabletop at her back.

"Thank you," she managed, but she didn't know if she was thanking him for retrieving the book or for the flowers. Although he hadn't exactly given her the flowers yet.

He passed her the bouquet then, and she held them gingerly, not quite believing someone had brought her flowers and equally not as sure what to do with them.

"I didn't wish to intrude upon the usual calling hours as I'd hoped to have a private conversation with you regarding my behavior last night." He seemed to wish to say more, but stopped, his eyes scanning the room around her before settling back on her. "Do you have a chaperone? A maid or companion?"

She shook her head. "There's never been a need for one."

His behavior? Of what was he speaking? She'd been the one to accost him with her proposal. He had acted the utmost gentleman, had even tried to refuse her claiming a rule about protecting debutantes, but then…

Last night in that cupboard. The way his breath had been hot and whispering across her ear. How he'd pressed her back against the wall, the nearness of his body, knowing just how close he was to…

She must stop this. He was still speaking.

"Where is your uncle?" His expression had grown curiouser she realized.

"He's taking a walk." He was closer than he had been that night in the carriage, and she could make out that faded line of freckles along the ridge of his brow. She suddenly wished to touch it.

"You're alone? And your housekeeper admitted me."

She tilted her head, struggling to follow his conversation. It was very distracting seeing him in…daylight. "I asked her to show you in. She was merely doing my bidding."

He shook his head. "Do you always see gentlemen alone?"

"The situation has never come up before." She tried to put her fisted hands to her hips and realized she still held the roses.

Her grip was, in fact, so tight on them she'd wrinkled the burlap that protected their stems. Turning to the table, she stacked a trio of books to make room for the roses, laying them gently down. Her fingers lingered longer than they probably should have, but the sight of flowers—flowers meant for her—was strangely mesmerizing.

"You said you wished to speak of your behavior last

evening." She faced him, forcibly willing her heart to stop its thudding in her chest, her mind to focus.

But she found his eyes on the roses. She followed his gaze and realized the fingers of one hand still toyed with the edges of the burlap wrapping. She snatched her hand away and forced an odd smile.

"Ransom? About last night?" she encouraged, hoping he didn't see her fanciful meanderings.

His gaze came back to hers, but it was clouded now as though other thoughts had intruded upon their conversation. She had never had such interaction with a gentleman before. Her usual company was books, and books were never this mercurial. She didn't know whether to focus on his expression or the changing color of his eyes. To say nothing of attempting to unravel his words.

"I shouldn't have trapped you in the cupboard like that, and I most certainly shouldn't have come between you and your business with Lord Crandall. I should only hope that you understand I had the best of intentions."

She held her breath, waiting to see if he would say more, if he would withdraw his intention to see their arrangement through, but he seemed to be waiting for her to say something.

She didn't know what to say, so she said what was on her mind. "No one has ever given me flowers."

A line appeared between his brows, and she regretted speaking. This back-and-forth business was terribly confounding, and as she had no experience with it, she feared she would always be left not knowing what to say and then saying the entirely wrong thing.

But then the line between his brows dissipated, the skin smoothing as his lips tipped upward in a soft smile. "I find that incredibly hard to believe. I expect you have gentlemen callers lining up every day to see you, and each carry a bouquet far more worthy than my meager offering. You don't need to protect my feelings, Alice."

Did he speak the truth or was he merely jesting? It needn't matter. His words had flooded her with a strange warmth. To think her so appealing as to attract a bevy of callers. How absurd. But maybe he really did believe it.

So befuddled by her own thoughts and the conversation entirely she hadn't realized he had leaned closer, not terribly much but enough to notice the small lines radiating from the corners of his eyes, to smell the coffee on his breath. God, it seemed as though he was going to kiss her.

Her heart tripped, and her stomach clenched, and she wished the table weren't behind her as the need to run away flooded her.

But then his eyes drifted from her face and his brow furrowed as he said, "Are those astronomy texts?"

Fear replaced the warmth she coveted, and suddenly she felt exposed. What was she to say? Her mother had taught her to be wary, to hide this part of her from others.

Unnatural.

The letter writer's words came back to her at the same moment her mother's voice sprang into her mind. This was it. Ransom would learn the truth about her and reject her. Rejection she was used to, but this was something else.

She cared about what he thought of her, and she hadn't cared what others thought in a very long time.

"Yes," she managed, unable to say anything else, but it didn't matter.

His attention had turned fully to the books strewn on the table behind her. He shifted the books, lifting their covers as though to study their titles. Meanwhile her heart thundered in her chest, and the muscles along her neck grew taut.

"Is this your work then?"

No. Every fiber in her body wanted to lie to him. Wanted

to tell him this was her uncle Herman's doing, but she couldn't lie to Ransom.

So she finally said, "Yes." And then, "It is."

Her heart slowed to almost nothing, and she wondered if she might faint.

He shook his head. "I never would have thought astronomical study interested you." There was a space then, a silence between words, and she filled that silence with the thing that haunted her.

Unnatural.

Unnatural.

Unnatural.

Only he didn't say anything of the kind. He said something completely extraordinary instead, and when he said it, he looked right at her, his blue eyes so terribly kind. "I really had you pegged for a mathematician."

* * *

He REALIZED he was somewhat disappointed by this realization.

He had truly thought her a mathematician with her exactness and efficiency. But the pile of books and papers before him quite clearly proved him wrong.

He tapped the cover of one of the books. "I take it your interest in astronomy goes beyond the names of the constellations."

For a moment it looked as though she thought he might strike her, her eyes were so wide, her body tense. The sight of her like that struck something inside of him he had thought long banished, but then she moved, sliding ever so carefully away from him as she regarded the books behind her.

"Yes, I'm trying to locate the first mention of a certain

comet. Its discovery seems to be one of debate." Her fingers moved idly to stack together some loose papers.

"The comet mentioned in this month's news sheet from the Scientific Scholar Society?"

Her head snapped up at this, her eyes wary and confused, and he found the enigma that was Alice Atwood grow murkier.

"You know of the Society?"

He shrugged. "I like to keep abreast of the scholarship such organizations attempt. It helps in my philanthropic work." He gestured to the table. "And what have you found?" he asked, trying to steer her back to the topic at hand.

His intent in calling upon Alice that morning was to convince her not to proceed with her scheme, but the damn woman had confounded him the moment he had stepped inside the room with her.

Her hair was loosened, sweeping along her cheeks, softening her features, and her feet were bare.

In the daylight, he could see she parted her hair in the middle, forcing back the long, dark strands into a tight twist low at the back of her head. But it wasn't like that this morning. Had something interrupted her toilette? Or did she wear it in this looser style when she thought no one would see her?

The small change had the greatest affect, and like finding an optical illusion, once seen he couldn't unsee it. Just the smallest piece of her armor had fallen away, and his suspicion that she hid behind her plain appearance strengthened.

But why was she hiding?

He leaned against the table, placing both hands flat on its surface. He smiled his most charming smile, the very one that had worked on London's coldest, most neglected wives. However, when he showered Alice with the same devastating smile, she backed away, her shoulders colliding with the bookcase behind her, sending a slim volume tumbling from the shelf. She didn't try to catch it. Instead they both watched it fall to the floor with a thud against the carpet.

When she looked back at him, her eyes were wide behind her spectacles.

She hadn't been wearing them when he'd entered, but he'd been too startled by her loosened hair to take in her face before she'd shoved them back onto her nose.

He couldn't figure out the heart of the game she played. She was confident enough to break a pitcher over a thug's head, and yet when asked about her scholarly intentions, she ran back into her den like a frightened hare. How could a woman be so confident and yet so afraid?

"I haven't found it yet, but I've only just started on the journals from the previous year, and I believe the discovery is actually two years old or more. I'm simply going backward chronologically to conduct a thorough examination of the research."

"I wouldn't expect anything less from you than a thorough examination." He tapped the cover of the book he'd retrieved once more before turning away from her, hoping if he put some distance between them, it would help her to relax, tell him more. "I expect also that you have some sort of intent when it comes to your studies." He'd paced to the other side of the sitting arrangement in front of the windows before he stopped and looked back at her. "What are your intentions, Alice?"

The question was thick with innuendo, and he wondered how she would take it. Her response was hardly surprising.

"I thank you for your interest in my personal pursuits, Ransom, but I believe our arrangement is of a professional sort." She wrinkled her nose. "Why are you here exactly? Is there an issue with the agreement we came to last evening?"

She was pushing the topic of the conversation away from herself. That was rather telling but not unexpected.

He straightened, dropping every pretense of charm. "Alice, are you certain about this? You're not committing yourself to this endeavor under duress, are you?"

Her shoulders snapped away from the bookcase as her chin went up. "I am not acting under duress."

He waited a moment, and her fists went to her hips. He turned away to hide his smile. If she weren't being forced to do this, there must be some other reason. But what was it? He couldn't get her to speak of her personal interests, so how was he to find out?

He turned in time to catch her studying the flowers he'd brought. Her eyes darted back to him immediately, and he wondered what that was about.

She'd taken such care to lay them gently on the table one would think he had handed her the rarest of diamonds and not some hot house roses.

He stopped his pacing and folded his arms over his chest. "I think if we are to conduct this affair honesty should be paramount."

"Honesty?" A single eyebrow came above the rim of her spectacles. "I should think I've been most honest with you. Have I not?"

"You've been blunt. There's a difference. I should like to know why you are undertaking this endeavor and what it is you hope to gain from it."

"I already told you it's an experiment. I'm a scientist, and I should like to analyze what it is that happens between a man and a woman. It's a simple enough proposition." Her eyes slid back to the bouquet of flowers, and he got the odd sense she was lying. Or if not lying, at least not telling him the whole truth.

"If all you should like to do is observe, you can hire an

escort for that I should think." The words were far crasser than he would have used with a lady, but Alice was not the kind of lady he often found in his company.

As it was, she did not balk at his words. In fact, she tilted her head as though she were considering it. "I suppose you are right. I hadn't realized I could hire someone for this." She came around the table now, and he marked how relaxed her shoulders had become. "Tell me more about escorts."

He backed away. "I'm not telling you about escorts."

"Why not? You were the one who brought it up. I should like to know more. Are there, indeed, male escorts?"

For all her brazenness, he forgot she was still a sheltered lady of rank. By her position in society alone, she was protected from the worst the world had to offer. He found himself sinking down onto the sofa behind him to get away from her as though distance might end this line of conversation.

"Yes, there are male escorts. They would, ostensibly, perform the duties I believe you are seeking." He tasted bile on the back of his tongue. Picturing Alice with an escort was worse than thinking of her with Crandall.

Her lips firmed as if she were mulling this over, and then, rather absently, she sat down on the sofa beside him. "So I could just hire one to do my bidding?"

He slid to the opposite end of the sofa. "You can, but I would advise against it."

She turned and placed her arm along the back of the sofa, leaning toward him. The position pulled her gown taut across her chest, highlighting every single curve there. She wore one of those loose gowns that women tended to wear in the morning before receiving callers, but it only served to emphasize her silhouette as the loose fabric molded to her body.

"Why are you always trying to protect me? Do you not

realize my reputation matters little, and I have no one to disappoint?"

Her words painted a lonely picture, and horribly, he found it a familiar one. "You say that, and yet I have met a sister who cares very much for you."

Alice blinked. "Yes, I believe she does care, but rather in an absent way."

There was nothing absent about the way he had witnessed Adaline Atwood interact with her sister, but again, he got the sense Alice was attempting to steer the conversation away from herself.

His suspicions were confirmed with her next question.

"Have you any siblings?" she asked, avoiding his overture.

"I'm afraid I'm an only child."

"How terribly sad."

"Not at all." He smiled to hide how the truth had stolen his breath. He was treading too closely to dangerous waters, but she didn't know that. He simply had to nudge the conversation in a different direction. Two could play at this game. "I see it as my parents having the wisdom to stop when they got it right." He spread his arms to gesture to himself, and the line between her brows paired nicely with the frown that came to her lips.

"You would think that." Her tone held no censure. In fact, she almost sounded mildly amused.

"So why is it you believe your sister cares for you in an absent manner? She married a marquess. That will surely reflect well on you." He swiftly sidestepped any further conversation about him and pressed his point.

Alice's eyes narrowed, and she pushed to her feet and paced away from him. "I'm not sure it has anything to do with me actually. My sister loves Ash."

Ransom shifted in his chair at the word, finding his throat suddenly tight. "I beg your pardon?"

Alice whirled about, her eyes suddenly intense. "Love, my lord. My sister loves Ash. She always has."

"But Ash loves someone else. Surely your sister knows that." The word *love* stuck in his throat like a fatty piece of meat.

"She is aware of it. As is most of the *ton*, I'm sure. Ash's infatuation with Lady Valerie is hardly a secret."

"Yet your sister would marry him anyway?"

She'd made it to the other side of the table again and leaned against it, shrugging her slight shoulders. "Of course. I've heard love can have such powerful effects. Even so much as to cause a woman to make a completely irrational decision."

"You believe love to be irrational?"

"I don't believe in love at all. That is. I don't believe in it as an emotion." She straightened, and her fisted hands went to her hips. "Quite frankly I find love to be rather perplexing."

His mind jerked as though her words had physically slapped him. He was perfectly content to not believe in love but knowing Alice did not believe in it as well...no, that couldn't be. There was too much to Lady Alice for her not to believe in love. Indeed, he could imagine what kind of partner she would make for a lucky gentleman someday.

Dear God, what was he thinking? He surged to his feet as if he could outrun his thoughts. He must move this conversation back to safer ground. As it was, he was still no clearer on Alice's objectives for her scheme.

He followed her back to the table littered with her work. "What is your intent here, Alice? Obviously you are interested in the subject of astronomy, and this is far more than an amateur hobby." He pointed to the open books on the table and the scattering of notes. "Why this business about seduction?"

Her eyes went to the piles of her research, and he thought

he saw her shoulders twitch. He watched her as her gaze strayed to where the flowers lay in the careful spot she had cleared for them.

When she finally looked up, her expression was cold and sterile. "I'm afraid my interest in astronomy *is* purely amateur. Besides I have found the field of scientific study is not always open to women." He caught on her words, filtering them through his own perception of the field, but she kept going. "I have my own reasons for seeking out your assistance."

Parts of what she said were lies, but there was something in what she said that hurt her. He wondered what it was and felt his stomach twist in sympathy for the pain she was only just keeping at bay. When the feeling deepened and his mind reached for a memory he had long tucked away, he forced his thoughts back to the present.

"I would caution you against being too optimistic. The field you wish to explore does not lend itself to careful observation."

"Do you think it too dangerous?"

"Far too dangerous."

"I disagree." She pursed her lips into a frown. "I shall see for myself what kind of power seduction has over the rational mind, and I shall do it in a completely removed and analytical state."

His eyes were drawn back to the yellow roses he had brought, and he felt as though their entire encounter was like a mirage. He couldn't tell which bits were real and which hid faltering truths.

But it didn't matter. He had learned what he needed to. Alice would not be swayed from her endeavor, but more there were reasons for her crusade she felt the need to hide from him. Reasons that would lead her to tempt a rogue and risk her reputation. He had only to find out what they were.

He shifted, drawing nearer to her but not touching her. When he should have stopped though, he kept going, his lips so very close to her ear, the scent of lavender drifting from that tantalizing hair.

"Removed and analytical?" he whispered, and he felt more than saw her eyelids flutter shut. He pressed closer and now he let his lips brush her ear, but only just enough, so little in fact as to leave her wondering if she had felt his caress at all. "I will take great pleasure in proving you wrong, Alice Atwood."

He left her then, not bothering to wait for her to regain her senses, satisfied his point had been made, but somehow feeling as though he hadn't quite won the battle.

He would win next time though. Of that he was certain. There was just someone he had to see first.

CHAPTER 4

*S*he wasn't sure how long she stood there.

Feelings were rising and falling inside of her like the water in the Thames. So much emotion all at once after hardly any emotion at all, and she was left floundering.

When she had embarked on this scheme, she hadn't counted on so much turbulence in her own person. She had projected everything outward as one did in an experiment. It was as though she were viewing her actions through a lens, an observer carefully removed. But that wasn't how it went at all.

At some point she must have resumed her seat at the table because she was sitting there when the door to the study opened again. She looked up, expecting Uncle Herman, but instead a young girl stood there.

Alice blinked, confused. "I'm sorry. Are you lost?"

The young girl's smile was effervescent. "I beg your pardon, my lady," she said with a small curtsy. "I didn't mean to startle you none. It's only Aunt—" She stopped, her words trapped behind her huge smile. "That is Mrs. Marble asked me to inquire about luncheon."

Alice blinked again, her confusion mounting. She wasn't hungry. The last thing she was thinking about was food right then, but if the girl was inquiring about luncheon, what time was it exactly?

Absently she pushed her hands through her hair, disturbing the chignon at the nape of her neck even more. "This is going to be rather rude, but who are you?" Alice finally managed, her gaze lingering on the girl.

She couldn't have been much older than seven and ten, slight of frame, with plain brown hair tied back along the sides of her head. But her smile took up so much of her face one couldn't help but smile in return.

The girl gave a curtsy again. "I beg your pardon, miss. Er, my lady. I'm the new maid, you see. It's my first post, and I'm learning as best I can."

Alice pushed to her feet. "We have a maid now?" The girl looked about confused, and Alice waved a hand. "It's quite all right. I don't expect you to answer that." How much had the Duke of Greyfair paid for Amelia? The sum must have been extraordinary. "May I ask your name?"

The girl curtsied again. It was awkward and slightly unbalanced, and Alice felt a pang of sympathy for the young woman. What would it be like to find oneself in a home that was not one's own? Learning a new skill under such pressure? Alice couldn't imagine it quite frankly.

But the girl's smile hid any trepidation she might have been feeling. "The name's Kathryn, my lady. Mrs. Marble is my aunt. She thought this would be a good position in which I could learn what's expected of a proper maid."

"There's just the two of us in this household," Alice said then, worry niggling at her. "Will that be enough for you to learn the duties of a maid?"

The girl's eyes went wide. "Oh, there's nothing to worry about there, my lady. I've already learned a great deal, and I only arrived this morning. I never knew it took quite so much to run a grand house like this."

Biggleswade House had been grand once, but Alice wasn't sure she would apply the term to its current state. She did feel her worry evaporate at the girl's eager face.

"That's wonderful," she said. "I take it you've met my uncle then as well? It's only the two of us in residence now, and I'm afraid we're both rather consumed in academia." She gestured to the table before her. "You may find many tables such as these throughout the house, and my uncle has a tendency to forget where he's laid things down. I'm afraid you must acquire the skills of a detective inspector before long." She'd meant it playfully, but as with most things of a jovial nature, she wasn't sure if it came out correctly.

As Kathryn's wide smile slid into a concerned frown, Alice was fairly certain she had missed the mark.

But then the maid shook her head. "It shan't be a problem, my lady. I've always been good at finding what's lost. Me mum is always saying so."

Alice nodded, pleased they had moved past her gaff. "I'm sorry. You came in here to ask a question of me. What was it again?"

How muddled were her thoughts that she couldn't remember a simple question?

"Mrs. Marble should like to know if you are interested in luncheon. She was going to lay some things out in the dining room if you were."

Alice turned to look at the clock on the mantel behind her at the same time her stomach gave a low rumble. She pressed her hand to it even though she was certain Kathryn was too far away to hear it.

"Luncheon would be lovely," she said, turning back to the maid. "I shall make my way to the dining room shortly.

Please tell Mrs. Marble it shall likely only be myself. My uncle's gone out for a walk."

Kathryn gave another curtsy, and Alice wondered if the girl didn't know when a curtsy was appropriate and had decided to do it frequently enough to pass muster.

"Of course, my lady." She moved to retreat through the door but stopped. "Should you like me to put those in a vase for you, my lady?" She held out one hand, pointing gingerly to the table in front of Alice.

Alice followed the line of the girl's gesture and found the yellow roses, still carefully tucked into the piles of books on the table. She had forgotten about them, and seeing them now sent a fresh wave of...something through her.

Happiness, elation, disbelief, trepidation—it was all awash inside of her.

"Yes, that would be lovely. Thank you."

Kathryn gave a firm nod and marched forward as though the flowers were the most important task she would attempt that day. "I shall put them in your rooms, shan't I? It's always nice to have a reminder of your beau's affections when you first wake in the morning, isn't it?"

"It is?" The words slipped from Alice's lips before she could stop them. She hadn't thought of where the flowers should go. It was enough that she felt a primal urge to protect them. She couldn't think beyond that.

Kathryn's smile wavered. "Oh it is, my lady." Her eyes narrowed as if in thought. "My lady..." The maid's voice had grown tentative. "Have you not received flowers from a gentleman before?"

It was an intrusive question and one Alice should have admonished the maid for, but at the moment, Alice was quite overcome with so many thoughts she knew the only thing to help would be to speak of them. Except she'd never felt such an urge in her life and when she finally did, both of her sisters were married and gone. What terrible luck. But Kathryn was here, and her smile was so friendly.

"No, I've never received flowers before." She kept her tone steady even as her heart pounded, and her fingers trembled.

Kathryn's smile returned in full force, and she scooped up the yellow roses, delicately holding them to her nose. "Oh, my lady, how exciting! Your first flirtation. There's nothing like it."

"There isn't?"

Kathryn shook her head and held her nose to the roses again. "Ach, there truly isn't. Tell me. Is he a handsome gentleman?"

Ransom's deep blue eyes flashed into her mind unbidden, and she said, "Yes," but the word came out as hardly more than a whisper.

Kathryn giggled. "Oh, how lucky you are then." The maid leaned closer, conspiratorially. "I always seem to attract the unfortunate ones. It's not so much their faces I mind. It's that they always seem to carry with them some truly awful smells. There was once a bloke that worked in the tannery." She leaned back, and her eyes widened as if in warning. "Never court a gentleman what's works in a tannery. My eyes wouldn't stop watering for weeks."

Ransom had a wonderful smell. Sandalwood and vanilla. He hardly made her eyes water, but that wasn't what was important just then.

"Kathryn, have you experience with gentlemen? I mean to say…well, this is rather awkward seeing as you're so young, but…" She didn't know how to finish the sentence, but it needn't matter. The maid seemed to understand what Alice intended.

"Oh, I've loads of experience. My pa owns the bakery down on Washbaum Street. It really draws in the suitors.

They all think my pa is going to leave the bakery to them." She laughed as though this were impossible. "They never stop to ask if I've a brother my pa has already trained to take over."

"And does he?" Alice's voice was nearly breathless, and she realized at some point she had become enraptured by this girl's story, a world away from her own and yet far more vibrant.

Kathryn laughed again. "Ach, of course. He may only be eight right now, but Bobby is going to grow up to be a fine baker. It's in his blood." The maid shook her head. "Men can be so silly sometimes." She held the roses. "I'll go see to these now and let Mrs. Marble know about luncheon then, shall I?"

She was already turning away when Alice called out to her. "Kathryn." She waited for the maid to turn back. "When you say your father's bakery really drew in the suitors, what do you mean by that?"

Alice was already inexperienced when it came to match-making, and the idea that Kathryn's father's bakery would have anything to do with it seemed somehow inconceivable.

Kathryn shrugged. "It's just that, my lady. When a gentleman decides to call on a girl, he's not only looking at her face and figure, now is he? He also wants to see what else she would bring to a marriage. And a bakery is a fine addition where I come from."

"Thank you, Kathryn. I appreciate the explanation."

The maid studied Alice for a moment, and she fought the urge to shift on her feet as the maid's expression grew cautious.

"Of course, my lady. I'm happy to answer any questions you might have," the girl said, her voice warming before she turned and left.

A gentleman doesn't only consider a woman's face and figure. Why hadn't Alice thought of that? Greyfair had married Amelia without even seeing her. Of course there would have been other considerations in the match.

Unnatural.

She dropped into her chair and picked up the nearest book, refusing to allow herself to count the marks mounting against her.

* * *

THE DOOR OPENED before he'd even had the chance to knock.

"My lord." The butler stepped back allowing Ransom entrance.

"Good day, Fredricks." He shed his hat and gloves. "I take it the master of the house is in."

"Always to you, my lord," the servant said with a barely perceptible warmth to his voice. He gestured to the drawing room off the foyer and disappeared to the back of the house.

Ransom didn't wait long before the sound of heels on the tile floor in the corridor beyond met his ears.

The person entered without greeting and instead went straight to, "Has your mother died?"

Ransom turned to face the woman in the doorway. "I'm afraid not."

The woman's expectant expression faded until only her oversized canines were visible at the edges of her wilted smile. "I suppose it was too much to hope for." She brightened again. "At least you're here. To what do I owe such a wonderful pleasure?"

She strode into the room then, hands outstretched as Ransom took them in greeting, squeezing his aunt's long fingers in genuine warmth as he kissed her cheek.

"I need to speak with you about a woman," he said when he drew back.

Her face fell again. "Oh God, I should think not." She

plucked her hands from his grasp and went to the corner to pull the bell pull. "I have no interest in your romantic escapades. You know I don't approve."

"It's actually not a woman I'm pursuing, and yes, you've made your stance on my lifestyle perfectly clear."

His aunt turned a knowing eye on him. "It's not that I don't approve of your lifestyle, Ransom. It's only you and I both know perfectly well you take up with these women to avoid answering some uncomfortable questions."

"Which questions are those?" he asked teasingly. His aunt was correct. They both knew of the void in his life left by his mother and Emma's sister-in-law.

His aunt returned to the center of the room where he lingered to flop onto the nearest sofa, her arms falling to either side of her along the back of the sofa. His aunt Emma was tall, especially for a woman, nearly six feet, and her arms seemed to engulf the sofa, shrinking the furniture with her very presence.

"Why is it that you try to run away from anything meaningful or God forfend, permanent and lasting?" She pursed her lips, screwing them up to one side as if to hammer home her point.

He didn't take the bait but instead dropped to the sofa opposite. "As much as I enjoy a philosophical debate, I'm afraid I haven't the time. I'm here to talk about your research."

She dropped her arms and sat up, bringing her face into the light that spilled through the large front window at his back. He was struck suddenly by the passage of time he found there in the little hashmarks beside her eyes and mouth that told of millions of smiles over many years. How had so much time passed?

His aunt Emma had been the one thing he could count on in his childhood and then a beacon in his tumultuous early adult years. But now instead of seeing the timeless conqueror always coming to his rescue, he saw a woman on the other side of sixty enjoying a quieter time in her life. Past children and marriage and settling into her golden years.

Except at the mention of her research, the fire that sparked to life in her eyes was not suggestive of a woman slowing down. "My research? Is this about the new observatory? Is there something wrong with the funding?"

He sat back on the couch, crossing one ankle to the opposite knee. "No, it's nothing like that. The observatory is on track to open as scheduled. This has to do with the other side of things."

She had dropped her hands in her lap when she sat forward, and now she shrugged, sending her hands dancing to opposite knees as if she couldn't contain the energy speaking of her research boiled inside of her. "What of it?"

"Do you find your work stymied because of your sex?"

Her brow folded, and her lips pursed again. "What has brought this up? Who is this woman you've encountered?" Her voice had taken on a note of incredulity, and he felt the slightest chafe at the tone.

Was it so hard to believe he might have met someone with whom he may have conducted a substantive conservation?

It was the same someone with whom he had shared two disturbingly powerful encounters, but that should hardly matter.

"Do you recall Ashfield Riggs?"

"The judge's son you met at Eton? You haven't spoken of him in some time."

He had already opened his mouth to answer her when the last bit unsettled him. "Of course I've spoken of him." Ash was his closest friend. He must have mentioned him to Aunt Emma from time to time.

But Aunt Emma shook her head. "We hardly talk of your pursuits, Ransom. You know as much. Especially of late. You're rather consumed with your goal to completely eradicate the scars your mother left on you through debauchery and women." She spoke the words as if she were listing items on a grocery order.

He felt the urge to defend himself, but it quickly died away. Aunt Emma was right, at least partly, and he couldn't summon the energy to sort through it.

"We've spoken of other things," he said instead. "The observatory is a prime example."

"Your philanthropic work is hardly discussing your personal pursuits. I know you've only agreed to be an investor for the observatory because of my own interests."

"You give yourself far too much credit. Lord Dalton would be wounded."

"Hardly," she said neatly. "The man may have good intentions in seeing to the building of the observatory, but his viewpoints can be dangerously narrow. Besides your interest in the matter only indicates you enjoy flattering me. So what is it this time that has brought you to my door? I can't imagine what this woman must be like. Do I know her?"

The string of words came so rapidly it was a second or two before he realized she had asked a question.

"I'm not sure. She's the Earl of Biggleswade's daughter."

For a brief moment, recognition flashed across Aunt Emma's features, but then her face died into a frown. "Oh, which one? Aren't there several?"

"There are three, in fact. I'm speaking of the youngest one."

She raised an eyebrow at this. "It isn't like you to dally with the younger set, is it?"

"I don't think that's relevant." His tone had gone flat, but it seemed not to affect his aunt.

She leaned back again, spreading her arms along the back of the sofa. "Oh, I find it an incredibly interesting point of data. Go on. What is this young woman's name?"

"Alice," he said without thought.

"You are familiar enough with her to use her given name then?"

He could feel the heat crawling along his neck, and at once, he wished to stand and leave the room. He'd never spoken of matters such as this with his aunt, and he suddenly felt squirmy. But he was saved from having to answer with the arrival of a maid and tea cart.

Aunt Emma slid forward on the sofa to pour as soon as the maid had departed.

"So please tell me about Alice," she said as she spooned sugar into a cup.

"Lady Alice Atwood is the youngest of the Earl of Biggleswade's daughters, and she has an interest in astronomy."

Aunt Emma looked up so swiftly from the teapot she nearly overflowed the cup. "Does she really? How peculiar."

"She had the Scientific Scholar Society's latest news sheet in her possession."

Aunt Emma's grip tightened on the teapot until he thought she risked shattering it in her grip. "Oh dear. Did she see that codswallop about the comet?"

"I believe she was trying to refute it."

Aunt Emma set down the teapot with a jarring thud. "She was what?"

Ransom felt another strange sensation pass over him, and for a moment, he thought he might be coming down with something. It almost felt as though he were betraying Alice's confidence. He had taken his time perusing her notes, and it was not as though she'd tried to stop him. But then she likely didn't know that he understood what it was he was reading.

"She had several of the journal's mentions of comets from past years. She's doing an investigation starting from two years ago."

The tea was entirely forgotten now. "And? What has she found?"

He remembered how he had seen her when he'd first entered the Biggleswade study. Her hair loose about her face, her bare feet sinking into the carpet, her face—God, he wished he'd been quick enough to see her face without those damn spectacles.

"I believe she's only just begun her investigation."

Aunt Emma sat forward. "But do you think she has the stamina to complete such a search?"

"Yes." He spoke the word without hesitation, and Aunt Emma straightened, her head going to one side as if in curious reaction.

"How well do you know this girl? I must say I'm only familiar with the beautiful one." She made a gesture with her hand. "The one sister who was out in society."

"Adaline," Ransom supplied.

"That's the one. I suppose she's the one who initially caught your eye." Aunt Emma gave a knowing smirk.

Ransom picked up the abandoned teapot to finish pouring himself a cup, the need to gloat almost overcoming his senses.

"It wasn't actually, but Adaline did play a role in it. I met Lady Alice at Adaline's wedding to Ash."

"Heavenly hosts, you must be joking." Aunt Emma's eyes widened, and he picked up her hand to place a teacup into it.

"I am not." He sipped at his own tea before continuing. "But I'm afraid I'm here for matters other than the comet."

"What's more important than the comet?" She turned abruptly, nearly upset her teacup to point at a table behind her, one that looked very similar to the one at which he'd found Alice. "I knew straight away when I read my own news sheet that it was absolute rubbish. That comet was identified ages ago."

"Lady Alice has asked me to seduce her."

Aunt Emma dropped the teacup onto the table in front of her, tea and milk sloshing everywhere. "Ransom."

He set down his own teacup more gently and held up both hands in placation. "I have no intention of doing so, but the woman seems bent on being ruined. I agreed to the matter to identify her true intentions and to stop her from making a careless mistake."

"How noble of you." Aunt Emma's dry tone was not lost on him.

"Not noble at all. It's rather a degree more terrible than that. I find the woman interesting."

"God forfend," Aunt Emma whispered, pressing a dramatic hand to her chest. "What do you intend to do about it?"

"That's why I'm here. I think Lady Alice has some kind of idea in mind that she hopes to achieve through this mad scheme. I've tried to flatter her, but she seems immune to my charm. She did, however, mention a recent submission of her studies to the Scholar had been rejected. I thought I should ask a fellow scientist how I may go about discovering her true intentions."

"Her true intentions? You mean she is attempting to discover something through seduction?"

"It's the only thing I can deduce."

"How interesting." Aunt Emma crossed her arms and placed her chin on one fisted hand. "I suppose she would approach it like one would approach any scientific endeavor. There must be a set of outputs she is hoping to study, and she believes the outputs would be uncovered in the scheme of seduction." She dropped her arms and met his gaze. "What kind of outputs would she wish to discover? I've never been particularly impressed in that field." She muttered these last words, her eyes traveling toward the ceiling, and Ransom supposed heaven beyond where her dearly departed husband might be resting.

"Do you think he can hear you from beyond the grave?"

She dropped her eyes. "If I thought he could, I would speak more loudly and enunciate. The old crow was always hard of hearing."

Ransom didn't bother hiding his smile. He knew his aunt did not have a love match in her marriage, but then she'd never been the type of woman to claim to want one. Her marriage to Viscount Wetherby had always seemed more of a camaraderie than any marriage Ransom had witnessed as a child. But then marriage had seemed entirely confusing to him thanks to his mother's actions.

"But if Lady Alice should seek to discover something through her seduction plan, I'm afraid you must go along with it in order to uncover the truth. You wouldn't want the poor girl falling prey to society's rogues."

"I am one of society's rogues."

She patted his knee. "Yes, but we all know you're just playing the part. You really haven't the heart for it."

"I think that's precisely the point."

Her hand stilled in the air as she went to withdraw, and she eyed him as though he had a spot of tea on his chin. "Is that what you think? That you haven't a heart?"

"My mother ensured that I did not." There was no accusation in his words. Too much time had passed for that.

She withdrew her hand entirely then, and she pressed her lips into a thin line, stopping any further words from spilling forth. But it needn't matter. Her expressive face prevented her from concealing her feelings on the matter.

He stood, deciding to ignore the topic entirely. "If I

should go along with Lady Alice's scheme to uncover her intent, do you have any words of advice about how I should go about it?"

Aunt Emma stood as well, her hands toying with her skirts as she seemed to consider his question. "I would approach it as she is approaching it. She wishes to uncover something in a scientific matter. You must play to her whims."

"Her whims?"

Aunt Emma's eyebrows went up as they often did when parlaying an important point. "You must seduce her scientifically."

"How terribly exciting," he mumbled.

CHAPTER 5

*S*tanding once more in the field of wallflowers at the edge of the ballroom, she wondered if she should be alarmed at how familiar she was growing with this situation.

She'd never been one to frequent balls with any regularity before, and now she had been to more than one since the start of her scheme. How dreadful.

But Ransom's note had been most insistent, and she'd been surprised to find an invitation to the very ball at which he'd requested a meeting on her uncle's desk. She'd responded in the positive and returned the invitation that morning after receiving Ransom's urgent note.

Now she stood, waiting.

She wondered momentarily if she'd gotten the wrong ball, but that was highly unlikely. She just didn't make mistakes with information like that. She checked the small watch pinned to her reticule. Nearly an hour had passed, and there was still no sign of him.

Not for the first time did she wonder what they were doing there. Seduction did not seem the thing one conducted in a ballroom, but perhaps she was mistaken about that. Such things were precisely why she was attempting this experiment.

If only her counterpart were taking the situation as seriously as she was.

She checked her watch again and then resolutely crossed her arms over her chest to avoid looking at it once more.

"Are you always this agitated or is it the thought of seeing me again that has you vexed?"

She did not start at the sound of his voice. She only turned and glared. "You're late."

His eyebrows rose. "I don't believe I stated a time in my note."

"The ball started over an hour ago." She realized then that he'd been reaching for her arm, and she'd stopped him somehow. Was it the tone of her voice or the intent in her words?

"One is never on time for a ball, my lady. It's not done."

A flush sprang up her neck unbidden, and she looked away. "I wasn't aware," she mumbled.

This explained the odd looks she'd been given by the baron and his wife when she'd arrived with Uncle Herman promptly at the time stated on the invitation.

"It's quite all right. No one really cares when one arrives at these things. It's only how one makes an exit that is noted."

She looked back swiftly at this, gesturing vaguely with one hand in the direction of the staircase. "The butler is announcing people when they arrive. How can you say such a thing?"

Instead of following the direction of her hand, he looked about them. "And precisely no one is paying attention to him."

It was she who followed his gaze and noted how exactly right he was. The guests around them were absorbed in their own conversations, hardly giving a care to what was happening around them.

"I see your point," she mumbled again before adjusting her reticule. "Now then. What is it that you wanted?"

Once more with the eyebrows. That was getting a touch annoying.

"Aren't we engaged in some sort of clandestine affair, or do I have that wrong?"

She was taken aback by the sudden heat that flamed her cheeks. "You do not have that wrong, my lord." She glanced about them, but no one was listening to them. Why should they? It was only Alice Atwood.

"I should like to speak with you further about the matter we discussed some days ago."

Five days. It had been five days since he had shown up at Biggleswade House. She'd counted every one of them, and she didn't know why. There was a strange compulsion inside of her that beckoned her to track the time that occurred from her last encounter with him. It had been five days. If she were being precise, it had been five days, eleven hours, and—she flipped over her wrist to see her watch hanging from the reticule—twenty-seven minutes and four seconds.

She dropped her wrist to find him staring at her.

"Do you have a prior engagement, my lady?" His tone was playful, and she wasn't sure how to respond.

"No, of course not. It's almost the middle of the night. Libraries will all have been closed for hours."

The light was soft in the corner they were backed into, but she would have sworn she saw him hide a smirk. She wasn't sure what she had said that had been so amusing, but Ransom had obviously taken delight in it. It wasn't as if he was mocking her though. It was almost that he found her... intriguing? No, that couldn't be.

"Then I should very much like this dance."

He took her arm before she had time to respond, and she found herself frozen to the floor. Her hand went to his, seizing his fingers as they lay wrapped around her forearm, her eyes intent on his face, and still the words did not come.

She realized dimly they were making a spectacle. The guests around them had turned to investigate the commotion, and there they were. Alice clinging to the Earl of Knighton's hand on her arm. This was not at all how this was supposed to happen, and oddly, she found embarrassment pooling deep in her stomach.

She thought she didn't care—*couldn't care*—what people thought of her. Not anymore. Not after what her own parents had done to her. But perhaps some instincts could not be overcome, and public embarrassment might have been one of them.

She did the only thing she could in that moment. She hissed, "I can't dance."

Ransom closed his opposite hand over hers. "I beg your pardon."

She glanced again at the guests milling about them, slow to proceed to the dance floor should they miss whatever transpired at the dangerous fringes of the ballroom.

"I can't dance," she said more forcefully. "I never learned how," she added, the embarrassment crawling up her throat.

Ransom straightened and—

Laughed.

A full, deep belly laugh.

The embarrassment crescendoed until it robbed the very breath from her lungs.

He was laughing.

He was laughing *at her*.

Pain. Actual physical pain. That was what she was feeling. Spreading through her body, overtaking her senses until she couldn't see anything but him.

No. This couldn't be happening. She shouldn't care what he thought of her. She was stronger than this. She had survived—

He patted her hand. "That could have been far worse."

Why was he speaking so loudly?

He turned away from her, toward the gawking guests. "She took a small spill, I'm afraid. Lucky I was here to catch her in time."

What? She hadn't tripped. What was he saying?

He smiled then, that smile that had captured the hearts of unsuspecting society matrons, the smile that had enraptured inexperienced debutantes. He was charming them like the rogue he was. She stood there, transfixed, watching as he cast his spell over the onlookers.

And then—

Nothing.

The guests who had been staring gave weak smiles then and turned away, having already forgotten her.

It was all moving too quickly. Her emotions were cartwheeling inside of her, one after the other, and she couldn't keep up with them.

He hadn't been laughing at her. He was...what? Protecting her? Defending her? Shielding her? Whatever it was, was so outstandingly unfamiliar to her, she couldn't name it.

"We'll have to be more careful as we promenade, shan't we?" He gave her a decisive look, and she found herself nodding.

"Yes, we shall." She removed her hand from his, allowing him to fully take her arm.

He didn't speak as they made their way around the dance floor. Eyes turned in their direction and quickly looked away once they saw it was only Alice Atwood on the Earl of Knighton's arm. She was sure of it.

How pitiful.

She had never before felt the storm of emotions a wallflower might even though she had been one since the moment she'd come out. This was the first time it was real, and she found she didn't care for it.

She glanced at Ransom, wondering if her feelings were due to the fact that it was him with whom she promenaded or that it was happening at all. She just couldn't be sure.

Unnatural.

She swallowed and let him lead her around the ballroom. She didn't speak. She didn't know what to say. What young lady didn't know how to dance? It was practically one of the first things they learned. But she didn't know how. Her mother hadn't thought it worth it.

The memory stung, and she shoved it aside. Her mother was dead. What she thought of her last daughter no longer mattered.

Except it did.

The voice whispered through her mind, and for a second, the letter writer's accusations seemed to meld with her mother's criticisms, and she couldn't tell who was who any longer.

Her thoughts must have carried her away because next she knew Ransom was leading her outside, through the terrace doors and down into the gardens. It wasn't at all scandalous. The terrace and the gardens just below it were well lit, and promenading couples filtered in and out of the ballroom. The music was muffled here, but she still caught the strains of the waltz, and her heart thumped harder.

"I'm sorry," she rushed to say. "I should have warned you. No, that's not it." She pulled her arm from his to press her fingers to her forehead, a slight pounding brewing there. She dropped her hand and faced him. "I'm sorry I don't know how to dance. We hadn't the money for it." The lie slipped readily from her lips because it was easier to speak than the truth.

He faced her, unmoving, and she wanted to squirm under his gaze. He'd never looked at her like that before. Ransom was always so charming, so playful. But he scrutinized her now as though he could see through her very skin.

"Could your family not afford it or did someone think such lessons would have been wasted on you?"

The muscles at her neck tightened at his words, but she stopped the gasp from escaping her lips and giving her away.

How could he have known?

He took a step closer to her, so close she could smell sandalwood and the hint of vanilla. God, why did he smell so good?

He was looking down on her now, much as he had done when he'd kissed her that night under the streetlamp. She looked up into his deep, deep blue eyes and wondered if she could disappear into them. Suddenly she realized how very much she wanted to because somehow, she sensed she was safe with him.

She wasn't sure when she had decided this, but it was only then that she realized it. Perhaps it was what he had done in the ballroom that had finally determined it for her, but she knew it now, understood it.

Ransom would never hurt her. She could trust him. Warmth flooded her, and her heart began to pound. She wanted to press a hand to her chest to stop it, but she couldn't move. He had captured her without even touching her.

"What happened to you, Alice?" He whispered the words, his eyes roaming over her face.

And then he was gone. He stepped back and away, and with a flourish, he bowed to her.

"May I have this dance, my lady?" he said, lifting his head to flash her a grin.

She started, an aborted laugh tumbling from her lips. "What?" she stammered. "I only just told you I can't—"

He straightened, his grin turning to a genuine smile. "But there's nothing stopping you from learning now, is there?"

They stood facing each other and dimly she was aware of the other couples filtering back into the ballroom. Soon it was just them down in the gardens and one other couple on the far side of the terrace. They might as well have been alone. The air was thick with midsummer blossoms, and the darkness around them was kept at bay by the lanterns strung along the terrace.

She picked up her skirts in one hand and curtsied ever so carefully. "I don't suppose there is, my lord," she said and took his hand.

* * *

WHY WOULD a young lady of society not learn to dance?

His first instinct told him it was Alice's own choice. He'd learned enough now to understand that she was not only stubborn, but she was determined as well. But whenever he thought along those lines, he recalled her quiet focus on the yellow roses he'd brought her. She had looked at them as though they were a delicacy she couldn't afford.

Had someone in her past told Alice she didn't deserve to learn how to dance? Had Alice been told it wouldn't be necessary? That no gentleman would court her, requiring her to know the steps?

He didn't like the tightness in his chest such thoughts caused. There was nothing at all wrong with Alice Atwood, but someone in her past had told her there was. And worst of all, she still believed it.

He wanted to unravel it, the damage that was done, and the thought itself was absurd but more that he should feel such altruistic intentions for a lady was preposterous. Aunt Emma was correct. He did enjoy charming women because it kept him from seeing deeper into his soul. His roguish ways masked the scars left on his heart from someone who should have loved him unconditionally.

The parallels were not lost on him as he held Lady Alice in his arms, but he chose to ignore them.

"You place your hand here at my shoulder while I place a hand here at your waist." He brought her hand to his shoulder before slipping his own about her waist. She was tall for a woman, and he didn't miss how perfectly she fit in his arms. It was really just a convenience. He wasn't going to think any more on it. "This is a waltz. Are you familiar with the music of a waltz?"

They stood at the edge of the light cast from the lanterns strung along the terrace, and the music was faint but still distinguishable against the night sounds of the garden. Its three-beat rhythm pulsed through the air, and he was certain she could feel it.

"I am," she said, her chin up even as her voice wavered ever so slightly.

It was funny, holding her like this. Their encounters had not been the sort he had had before. He was used to luxurious bedchambers and plush settees. When it came to Alice, he always seemed to be stealing a touch, capturing an embrace. Even now he struggled to keep his feet even in the soft, damp grass.

How was it so difficult to seduce a woman who very clearly wished to be seduced?

That part of him he was trying so resolutely to ignore tugged against his conscience. He knew he had been unable to hide his curiosity about Alice Atwood from his aunt, and now he couldn't deny it to himself. Everything was different about Alice, and suddenly he wanted different because the things he had used to distract himself from his past before were no longer working.

"And can you feel the three-part movement to the music?"

She blinked, her eyes almost unreadable behind her spectacles in the near darkness. "I don't understand the words you just said."

"Have you never listened to music before and felt it move you?"

"I've never listened to music before. I find the subject tedious."

If anyone happened upon them now, he wondered what they might think. They were only standing there in the grass, arms about each other as if to begin a dance they were to never start. But he didn't think on it long as he tried to unravel what she was saying.

"How is it tedious?"

Her lips thinned, and he remembered that first night when she had accosted him in his carriage. He hadn't realized then how many of her emotions played over her face, but he was beginning to read her with greater ease. She was struggling now with how to put into words the things she understood so readily within herself.

"I've always heard others speak of music as though it were some sort of living thing that one creates from an instrument. I don't understand how that's possible when the object itself is inanimate."

"Ah, I see the problem." He adjusted his grip on her hand as he took two steps back, widening the distance between them. "No one has taken the time to mathematically explain music to you then."

Even though it was dark, he didn't miss the flash of curiosity in her eyes nor the subsequent guardedness that overcame then. Not for the first time did he wonder what had caused Alice to be such a dichotomy of emotions. She was eager clearly, but it was as though anything presented to her might contain a trap meant to harm her.

"What do you mean mathematically?" Her eyebrows hovered over her spectacles as she watched him.

"Music is nothing but an arrangement of fractions. Each measure—the units of music—is further divided into notes. It's very similar to how distance might be measured. Can you picture it?"

"The notes are the segments contained in the music? Like inches inside of feet?"

"Yes, precisely." He dropped his gaze to their feet, and she followed suit. "Now then, you move your feet according to the fractions. In a waltz, the musical measure is divided into three. Listen for a moment."

He stood perfectly still as he watched her. She looked past his shoulder in the direction of the ballroom as if she could see the music spilling from it and after a moment looked back at him.

"I can hear the three parts." Her voice was overly bright, and he wondered if she used the same tone when discovering something in her texts.

He smiled. "Exactly." He adjusted his grip on her again, pulling her closer this time. Her eyes never left his face, and he could feel the surprised breath she sucked in as he brought them together. It was at that moment he would have smiled. He would have poured on the charm and had the woman melting in his arms.

But he didn't do that with Alice. He simply liked holding her, watching her emotions unspool naturally, just the way she was.

He swallowed, pushing the unusual reaction deep inside

of him before saying, "Now we move our feet in time with the three-part movement. Like this."

He guided her with the hand at her back, applying just enough pressure to lead her smoothly into the dance. As soon as he took a step though, her eyes dropped to their feet, and she stumbled.

"Have you made any progress in your research on the comet?"

Her eyes flashed to his, huge and round, behind her spectacles, and her feet straightened out, following his without her breaking eye contact.

"My research?" For likely the first time since meeting her, her voice faltered, and he found it curious. If anything, he would think she would speak more confidently about a subject that interested her.

"Yes, about the comet in the Scientific Scholar Society's news sheet. I spoke about it with a friend who shares a similar interest, and we're agreed that you may be on to something."

Her feet stopped entirely, and he was left holding her. The music died softly as if the musicians somehow understood the dance lesson had faltered, but she didn't step back, didn't remove her hand from his shoulder. She only studied his face, her lips parted just enough to tempt him with the thought of a kiss.

"The comet? You wish to know about my research?"

"Yes, I do." He was the first one to shift, but it was only a movement of his feet as a degree of uncomfortableness passed through him at her scrutiny. He didn't let go of her though. He liked the feel of her in his arms. He knew that. Had known that since that first night under the streetlamp. "I have an interest in astronomy remember. I shouldn't say it's as great as yours, but I'm a keen observer."

"You are?"

He wondered what had happened, if his nearness had suddenly reduced her vocabulary. "Yes, I—" He stopped as soon as he realized what he was about to say. His eyes traveled over her face, turned up to his expectantly, and the words came forth anyway. "I'm a benefactor of the new observatory at College Park. Perhaps you're aware of it."

She did step back then, and he regretted his words. But oddly, she didn't let go of him. It was as though she'd forgotten she still held him. Her hand slipped from his shoulder, sliding down his chest to curl into the lapel of his dinner jacket while the hand he held dropped, her fingers curling into his until he was simply holding her hand.

It was like watching a knot tighten, the rope carefully laid but with one subtle movement the space between them disappeared. He swallowed, aware his heart had started to race with trepidation, knowing he should step back, but instead, he curled his fingers into the small of her back, holding her steady.

"You donated to the construction of the new observatory?"

"Of course. A new observatory was critical in the progression of the field here in London."

Her fingers curled tighter around his lapel, and he knew it would be irreparably wrinkled, but he didn't care. Simply standing there conversing with Alice Atwood was the most interesting thing he'd done in a long time. That should have caused him greater concern than a wrinkled jacket, but he couldn't even summon the proper agitation for that.

"The progression of the field? You speak as though you are aware of its developments."

He shook his head, trying hard to tamp down his smile at her eagerness. "I'm afraid I'm not directly involved. Merely a curious bystander."

"Curiosity is important in scientific research. If it wasn't for an unhealthy amount of curiosity, we wouldn't have lobsters, would we? Can you imagine the first person to eat a lobster? Someone looked at one of those creatures and thought I bet that would be delicious with butter." She shivered, her lips turning down. "Frightening creatures, but it says a lot about the power of curiosity."

He laughed, the sound loud and fragile in the quiet of the night, and he wasn't sure who was more surprised, he or Alice. But her face changed then, and her grip on his lapel loosened. A whisper of alarm went through him, and he realized he didn't wish for this moment to end. This moment that held just the two of them and nothing else.

But then she said, "Are you laughing because you mean it or because you wish me to think I'm amusing?" Her eyes had become guarded, and she watched him now, not with the intensity she had shown when he was attempting to teach her the steps of a waltz but with a wariness he was starting to understand she had learned from somewhere.

"Why would you believe my amusement isn't genuine?" He kept his tone low, careful, as he studied her face.

She said so much with her expressions, and if only he kept his patience, he could learn more than her words ever told him.

She shifted, her eyes dropping momentarily as if she were gathering her courage. "Earlier in the ballroom, you laughed to make those people think what you wished them to think. It made me realize I can't ever be sure what you truly mean and what is an act."

Her words were like a finger prodding a wound, and it was as though he flinched internally. It came easily to him now, making people think what he wished them to think, but when Alice pointed it out to him, it was startling to know others could see it.

Not for the first time he wondered if he was losing what

was left of himself, the true part of himself, the part he had left behind when he'd finally given up hope of his mother ever returning. Ever coming back for him. The part he only allowed his aunt Emma to see now but the same part Alice so easily discovered and beckoned to the surface.

It was so tempting. The allure of being himself. Of letting down the act for just a moment. Maybe then he could breathe.

He studied her face, the moonlight glinting off her spectacles, and he wondered once again what she looked like without them.

In the end, he let go of her, his hands dropping to his sides.

"With you, Alice," he said, his voice hypnotically low, "it's always real."

He raised his arms, cupped her face in his hands, and kissed her.

CHAPTER 6

*T*here was something different about this kiss.

The first one had felt pointed and urgent but not this one.

This one was slow as if he were holding back, prolonging it.

Savoring it.

That only made her want it more.

This may have been her second kiss, but she still didn't know what to do. The benefit of the urgency in the first one was that she wasn't required to know what to do. The tempo of the moment precluded her from needing to.

But now it was as though he were evoking a response from her, drawing her out as if he were hypnotizing her with a spell.

For a second she thought of that moment in the ballroom when he had so easily manipulated the guests into thinking what he wanted, and she couldn't help but wonder if he were doing that again.

Except then he closed the distance between them, his

body coming flush against hers, and he groaned, the sound so delicate, so pure, it was impossible not to believe.

He used his thumbs to push her chin up, slant his lips across hers, and then he was taking instead of savoring. Her hands came up of their volition, grasping his wrists just so she had something to hold on to.

Were those her toes curling in her slippers? Her stomach clenching as the desire inside of her built? Oh God, her knees were weakening. She could feel it, her legs had suddenly disappeared beneath her, and—

He was moving her.

How his arms had come around her, she didn't know, but he had lifted her against him just enough to move her. He was trying to get them away from the view of the terrace doors. He didn't want them to be caught.

Such care was alluring, but then maybe he wasn't doing it to save her reputation, but his. London's most successful rogue wouldn't be caught with a wallflower.

The thought cut through the fog his kiss had conjured, and she pulled away from him, willing her senses to emerge and see the situation for what it really was.

Only when she opened her eyes, she saw his face and forgot what she had been thinking. He had pulled them back into the darkness at the side of the terrace, and the rough stone of the house itself pressed into her back as he sheltered her in the shadows. But moonlight cut a swath directly over his face, illuminating him as if he were a star himself.

And nothing about his face suggested this was a charade.

The intensity of his eyes told her he was feeling as much torment as she was. The cavalier lightness of his expression from that moment in the ballroom had vanished, and in its place, she saw the man instead of the facade of the rogue he was supposed to be.

He didn't speak. He only watched her as though he were

memorizing her features. Pain erupted in her chest as the scars of her past were ripped open, exposing a wound she had thought long healed.

He saw her.

She could feel it. For the first time in maybe forever, someone was actually seeing her, and it hurt. It hurt to understand how much she longed for someone to see her.

He kissed her again, and she welcomed it. She welcomed the way physical touch seemed to obliterate everything else, and for a moment, she could forget the other part of it. She didn't want to think about whether or not this was real or what the intensity of the feelings he conjured in her meant. She wanted only his kiss.

His hands cupped her cheeks again, his thumbs pushing her head back against the rough stone. She held on to him, her fingers curling into his jacket at his waist, the only thing she could think clearly enough to grab hold of. His lips were gone as soon as they came, moving along the line of her jaw and down.

He pressed his mouth to her neck, and she came up on her toes, scraping along the rough stone at her back.

"Ransom." She didn't know where his name came from, but it slipped from her lips like an oath.

His hands left her face, skimming down her shoulders, pushing at the sleeves of her gown until one shoulder came free. His mouth chased his wandering hand, his lips burning a path from her neck and along her shoulder. Her fingers curled, dragging him closer to her, pressing her body to his.

The pulsing began low in her belly, so strong and sudden, she gasped.

He left her shoulder, his lips moving down, tracing a line along the edge of her bodice. Surely he wouldn't—surely he couldn't—

His mouth settled at the top of her breast, just at the edge of decency.

Decency? What decency? He was ravaging her in the shadows. There was nothing decent about what they were doing, and yet she felt as though he were holding back. It was torture. That's what he was doing to her. A sensual kind of torture that showed her what he could do to her without showing her everything.

No wonder he was such a successful rogue.

She didn't want to think about that. The realization struck her, and her fingers curled again, pulling him close as if she could shut out reality.

She wanted it to be just him and her and nothing else in that moment, and it should have frightened her. She had spent her whole life pushing others away to keep herself safe, and now she wanted nothing more than to be lost in that moment with him forever.

He moved again, traveling back up to her neck and farther, his lips coming to her ear as he whispered, "Do you have any idea what you do to me?"

He could have said anything at all, anything but that. Anything else she could have dismissed as flowery words meant to seduce her, but what he'd actually said was far worse. Because it made her wonder what, in fact, she did do to him. Was he feeling the maelstrom of emotion she was? Or was he used to this? God, had he encountered something—someone—better?

The thought had the desire cooling in her stomach, her muscles going rigid with apprehension.

What if he wasn't enjoying this? What if this was all for show?

What if the letter writer had been right?

And then he stopped. His lips left her skin, and his forehead came to rest against hers.

"What happened right there?" His voice was no longer thick and sultry but rather calm and soft as though he were speaking to a frightened kitten.

She did not appreciate the image.

"Nothing happened. Whatever do you mean?"

He leaned back, his eyes meeting hers. The moon had shifted somewhere behind them, and it cut a beckoning path across his face. It was as though the very stars she studied were giving him their blessing.

"You're a terrible liar, darling." His tone was rich with warmth now, and a grin played at the corner of his lips. "I could almost feel the gears in that incredible brain of yours turning. I hate to ask what it is you were thinking about as I would hope my attentions would make you unable to think at all."

She had stopped paying attention halfway through his words. "My incredible brain?"

Now the grin came into full effect. "Well, isn't it? I can't be the first person to have noticed."

The desire that had simmered low in her stomach just moments before turned swiftly to hard coal, and she fought the bitter taste it left in her mouth.

She dropped her gaze away as she answered, "I'm not sure it's all that great actually." She'd hardly mumbled the words, but his finger propped up her chin, forcing her to meet his gaze even when she didn't wish to.

"You're lying again, darling. Are you so uncomfortable speaking about yourself in such a way?"

"I'm not accustomed to speaking of myself at all." It was another lesson she had learned early. Speaking of herself as little as possible gave her mother far less ammunition with which to hurt Alice.

His eyes swept back and forth over her face, and she

wondered for what he searched. It was still the same face, and frankly, there wasn't much to look at there.

"Then I return to my earlier question. What happened when I was kissing you?"

He said it so plainly as though he were speaking of the weather, and yet she squirmed with the delicateness of the subject.

"Nothing happened." She tried to pull her chin from his finger, but the damn man moved his thumb, capturing her face in the lightest of grips. Her uncomfortableness turned to frustration. "Let go of me."

"Tell me the truth and I will."

"Let go of me, and I shall."

"No, you won't. If I let go of you, you'll retreat back into yourself again."

"I do not—" But he was right, and she didn't wish to finish that sentence. So instead she said, "I don't wish to say."

"So something did happen. What is it?"

She shook her head but only a small degree as he never loosened his grip on her chin. "I don't wish to say."

She couldn't be certain in the moonlight, but it looked as though his eyes clouded with concern. "Was it something I did? Something you didn't like? You must tell me, so I don't—"

"No, it wasn't anything like that. It—" Shame burned through her, stealing the rest of her words. She pulled on her chin, but his grip only tightened.

"Tell me."

"I don't want to look at you when I do."

"I want you to look at me."

The shame burned hotter, and a lifetime of disappointing others threatened to consume her. So she snapped her eyes shut and spoke as quickly as possible. "No one has ever found me pleasing in any sort of fashion, and your words confused me because I can't imagine having any kind of effect on you as good as the one you are having on me." She squeezed her eyes shut tightly then, the words floating somewhere just beyond her senses, and she braced for the moment he would walk away from her.

The first thing to go was the hand at her chin. It fell away almost immediately, and the night breeze suddenly swept over her face. She hadn't realized it had grown so cold.

Carefully she opened her eyes. He was still standing there, watching her. It was such a shock she reared back in surprise, bumping her head against the rough stone behind her.

"May I call on you tomorrow?"

"What?" She pressed her hands into wall behind her, its rough surface grounding her.

"Tomorrow. May I call on you? There's somewhere I'd like to take you. Do you have the afternoon free?"

What was he saying? She had just stripped herself bare before him, and he…wished to…

"Take me somewhere?"

He nodded once, efficiently, any suggestion of the rogue he had been moments before having suddenly vanished, and she wondered if there was something far deeper wrong with her than the accusations laid at her feet by the letter writer.

"Yes. If you're available."

Her head spun. The brusqueness with which he spoke, and the careful way he held himself was at war with the tumble he had made of her thoughts and feelings in the past hour.

"Yes, I'm available," she heard herself say.

"Lovely. I shall see you tomorrow then." He stomped off without another word.

When he passed the corner of the terrace, the moonlight struck him fully, and she saw how he held his hands curled into fists. She straightened away from the wall, but she didn't move for several minutes. Her slippers were soaked through with dew by the time she finally made her way back to the ballroom, but she wasn't any clearer on what, exactly, had just happened.

* * *

BEFORE LAST NIGHT, Ransom would have said he wasn't the murdering type.

Now he wasn't so sure.

His likely victims were unfortunately dead, which was probably for the best. They probably weren't worth the effort anyway.

He had met Adaline, Alice's oldest sister, at both the wedding and in society, and he was fairly certain she was not the culprit. For one, she smiled entirely too much. Someone who smiled that much could not subject her sister to such prolonged and aggravated cruelty.

For that was the only thing he could think of that would cause Alice such devastating insecurity.

If he closed his eyes, he could still see her, pressed against the wall, her body so tense as if she were afraid to relax even a single muscle for if she did, she would simply cascade into a million small, irreparable pieces.

His stomach lurched, and he did close his eyes, laying his head back against his chair. He'd retreated to his club that morning after a fitful night's sleep. It was still a couple of hours before he had to retrieve Alice, and he hoped the quiet bustle of the club would be distraction enough from his own thoughts.

No one had found her pleasing.

The headache brewing along his brow would suggest otherwise. He had pleasured many women in his tenure as a rogue. It was a tricky thing being a rogue with morals. He never dallied with women who did not invite his attentions, and after ten years, he had no need to seduce a woman now. They came to him, and he gave them pleasure. He had always seen his life in the positives it gave. Desperate women felt a relief of their loneliness if only for a time, and he kept the echoes of his past at bay.

But he'd never dallied with debutantes.

He pictured Alice, those damn spectacles obscuring her features. It wasn't as though he were breaking one of his few rules now. Alice didn't feel like a debutante. She didn't act like one either.

So why was he hesitating?

Because there was something fragile about her. It was in the way she watched him. Sometimes he felt not unlike one of her experiments, and she was waiting to observe some sort of reaction.

And she had caused plenty of those in him over the course of their acquaintance.

But he had told his aunt the truth. He wouldn't ruin her. No matter what she asked of him he would remain true to his principles.

At least, he hoped he would.

After the previous night's encounter, he was worried he might not be able to live up to his promise. God, she was like a powder keg going off in his hands. There was so much pent-up desire in her, and he thought it very likely she didn't even realize it. She was sensual without trying, alluring without being intentional. It was driving him mad.

"Knighton, is that you?"

He opened his eyes without picking up his head. He blinked a few times to bring the gentleman before him into focus. The man stood a few feet from Ransom's chair, a walking stick in one hand, a folded newspaper in the other, arms extended as though the sight of Ransom himself had suddenly stopped the man.

He looked vaguely familiar. One of those gentlemen Ransom had likely seen at some social function or in Parliament. One of a thousand faces he saw over and over again with little effect.

"Viscount Weare," he said as a name finally clicked with the man before him.

Weare was a younger chap, likely in his midtwenties, with sandy hair and bushy sideburns giving him an air of wisdom his age would not have suggested. But he was a nice young man, Ransom thought, quiet but not afraid to speak the truth.

His gaze now though was cloudy and confused.

"Is there something amiss?" Ransom asked. He could admit to being rather foggy from lack of sleep, but he looked around to make sure he was in the correct club. Whatever reason did Weare have to look at him with such confusion?

The man straightened, tucking the newspaper under one arm to grip his walking stick in both hands, idly twirling the thing between his palms.

"It's just I didn't expect you to stay in London. What with everything that has happened and such."

Ransom blinked. "What's happened?"

He knew he'd been spending too much time with Alice. He'd let some of his other prospects fall to the wayside, but it wasn't as though he couldn't pick up where he'd left off when he was done with Alice.

He nearly bit the inside of his cheek at the thought. Thinking about not seeing Alice every day suddenly seemed rather dull and uninteresting. God, what was happening to him?

Weare relaxed onto one foot, his posture curious now instead of confused. "With Ridgeway returning from Paris. I think a wiser man would have left London by now." The viscount's tone was one of joking camaraderie.

Ransom picked up his head. "Ridgeway?" He recalled the name. He'd had a rather arduous encounter with a Lady Ridgeway earlier that season. It had been fun, and he was certain the lady had enjoyed it. She had been exceptionally vocal about that.

Weare's face opened into a mask of concern. "Have you not heard then?"

Ransom sat forward in his chair, his hands going to the arms as if he instinctively knew to brace himself. "Heard what?"

Weare looked about them as if they might be overheard, but as it was everyone else seemed to know what Ransom did not, he wasn't sure it was worth the discretion.

"Lord Ridgeway is returning to London to call you out."

Oh bloody ballocks. Honestly, Ransom had expected such a thing much earlier in his career as a rogue, and he was quite surprised it had taken this long. He collapsed back in his seat, running a hand over his face.

"When exactly was Lord Ridgeway supposed to have left Paris?"

Weare shrugged. "I first heard the news probably two days ago."

Ransom dropped his hand, letting it fall uselessly to the arm of the chair again. "Two days ago?" Why hadn't Ransom heard this news by now? It seemed someone would have been eager to drop such a morsel at his feet.

Except he hadn't been circling in society the past two days. He'd been hiding in shadows with a delectable woman.

Jesus, he needed to get a hold of himself.

Weare shrugged again. "I heard it from the boys down from Cambridge. We were going for a row, and they—are you all right?"

Ransom hadn't realized he'd let his emotions come to his face. He stood and slapped the viscount heartily on one shoulder.

"I'm fine, mate. I thank you for letting me know of my coming demise." He smiled, but Weare's expression remained dubious.

"You don't sound concerned." Weare looked about them. "A man is coming to challenge you to a duel for impugning the honor of his wife."

Ransom straightened his jacket. "The same man who has been living in Paris the past year with his French mistress. I find the man's stance on values rather confusing, don't you?"

Weare only blinked. Ransom slapped him on the shoulder again.

"Thank you, Weare. I'll let you know if I should need a second." He walked away before the poor man could respond.

He would have walked to retrieve Lady Alice if he wouldn't subsequently need his carriage to take her to their outing. As it was, he allowed himself the indulgence of pouting from within the shadows of his conveyance as it rocked its way toward Biggleswade House.

Lord Ridgeway was finally returning to London to call him out. What hogwash. The hypocrisy was nearly suffocating. The man deserved to be cuckolded. He was the one who had abandoned his wife to live with his mistress in relative comfort in the margins that were the Continent.

Ransom knew perfectly well the problem with Ridgeway was not the cause of his grumpiness just then, but it was fun to indulge in it none the less. It distracted him from what really plagued him. At least for the time being.

The indulgence ended when they arrived at Biggleswade House, and the carriage door opened before his tiger had a chance to jump down and open it properly.

He sat back as Alice herself clambered inside, reticule bouncing threateningly against her skirts as she attempted to gain a seat. He eyed the bag suspiciously, wondering what she might be concealing today.

She dropped to the opposite bench with a flounce of her skirts.

"Lady Alice," he said, taking in the rest of her costume.

It was another drab gray gown of an indeterminable fabric. Something plain and serviceable. Her hair was pulled tightly under a small unadorned cap, and she shoved her spectacles up her nose just as his eyes reached her face.

"Lord Knighton," she said.

"I believe it's customary for a gentleman to escort the lady from her house."

She wrapped her hands around her reticule. "I saw no reason for such frivolity. I should like to know where we're going today."

"You'll see." He made to rap on the ceiling to let his driver know they could continue when Alice held up a hand.

"Wait," she said, her eyes darting to the door, which he realized was still open.

Vaguely, he heard hurried footsteps on the pavement outside, and then oddly enough another woman clambered her way inside the carriage. She smiled widely as she dropped onto the bench beside Alice, but otherwise didn't say anything.

"I've asked my maid to accompany me."

"Your maid?"

He studied the girl sitting next to Alice, and had he been pressed, he couldn't be sure he would have been able to tell which of them was the servant. If anything, he would have thought the maid the lady as she had fine porcelain skin, wide eyes, and a bright smile. Her dress was a pale lavender with small flowers embroidered along the cuffs. It was almost vibrant next to Alice's gray, and the tableau the two women made had his heart squeezing.

Not for the first time did he wonder why Alice dressed as she did, and not for the first time did he wonder if he was getting into something he shouldn't.

"Yes," Alice said then. "I thought it would be wise to bring a chaperone."

He shut his mouth and rapped on the ceiling to signal the driver to move on. He could not fault Alice for her logic there. His only worry was that a chaperone wouldn't be enough.

CHAPTER 7

*R*ansom was grumpy.

She had never seen him like that, and it sparked an unusual concern in her. It wasn't like her to be overly worried about a rogue. Although, to be fair, she hadn't the pleasure of knowing many rogues over whom to be concerned. But something was bothering Ransom, and she wished to know what it was. Except she felt Kathryn's smile beside her and decided it was probably best to hold her tongue.

Alice wasn't used to being in the company of servants, but she knew enough to keep private matters private. It wasn't that she didn't feel an instant trust when it came to Kathryn, but rather, it was that the maid was young. Alice didn't want to be the person responsible for dimming the young woman's view of the world.

She felt her heart lurch at the thought, and not for the first time, she wondered what kind of a person she would have been had it not been for her parents. If she were somehow magically born to another set of parents, another set of circumstances in which she wasn't the reason her father's last hope for a son was dashed, in which she wasn't the failure her mother despised. Would she now be sitting in a carriage with the rogue with whom she had struck a bargain to seduce her?

"You still haven't told me where we're going, my lord," she said, settling her reticule in her lap.

"I'm taking you to a meeting."

"I'm sorry?" She hadn't been expecting that. She'd prepared herself for a promenade, an exhibit, a show, or God forbid, even tea with a dear friend. A meeting was not at all an inkling in her mind.

"I'm taking you to a meeting. It's a group that I think you'll find most…" He let his voice trail off, and she found herself leaning forward, waiting for his next words.

Did rogues have some sort of club? Was he taking her to some establishment of ill repute? Oh God, what had she gotten herself into?

"Enlightening." He said the single word slowly with a great deal of innuendo, and then—and then!—he winked at Kathryn. Winked at the poor girl.

She forced herself to loosen her grip on her reticule lest she rip it to shreds. "Enlightening? My lord, I think perhaps there's been a misunderstanding." She glanced sideways at her maid who most definitely was already caught in Ransom's snare. "I should not wish to—"

"Lady Alice, did you not request of me services of a personal nature?" When had his eyes turned so molten? Only moments before she was convinced he had a thorn in his bottom for the darkness that overcame his features. But now —now he was…

Lud, he was a rogue. That was what he was, and he was spoon feeding her his act. She sat back, plopping the reticule in her lap, refusing to fall victim to his charm.

"You're in a strange mood today, Lord Knighton."

He'd been smiling at Kathryn, but his face lost all its warmth at her words.

"Strange? I doubt that very much."

She gave a noise of disagreement before turning her attention to the window, prepared to ignore him for the rest of their journey.

Which lasted precisely three seconds.

The carriage lurched to a stop, and the door popped open, the tiger placing the stool on the pavement and offering his arm even before Ransom delivered a retort. She knew he was about to. It was obvious from the way his lips pinched as if he held back speech.

She nodded for Kathryn to exit first as she was on the pavement side of the carriage, and Alice was not about to climb over her. Kathryn did as indicated, thanking the tiger for his arm as she descended.

Ransom moved to make way for her, but she seized his arm and yanked him close.

"What is wrong? You look as though someone has taken away your toy," she whispered, glancing in the direction Kathryn had gone only to find her smiling and laughing with the tiger.

When she returned her attention to Ransom, she found an expression there she hadn't seen on his face before. One of quiet contemplation as though he had just realized something.

"What is it?" she whispered again, but he only shook his head.

"Just a problem I must figure out."

She studied him a moment longer and finally released his arm, sure she would not get any more information from him and not a little worried she might be the problem. Not wishing to delve further into that with him, she made her way to the door.

She stopped on the pavement, her hands fisting in her skirts as she stared about them.

"This is Mayfair," she fired at Ransom like an accusation as soon as he made his way out of the carriage.

He too stopped on the pavement and looked around. "Do you know, I think it is?"

She didn't have the required muscles to frown at him to the degree she wished to. "Where are we?"

"Mayfair. You just said as much." He took her arm and led her up the set of stairs of the townhouse directly in front of them.

When he didn't knock at the front door but simply let himself in, she felt a lick of trepidation that this might really be some kind of scandalous gathering of rogues. In her mind flashed an image riddled with petticoats and crinoline and lecherous old men and—

"Ransom, what are you doing here? You know men aren't allowed—" The woman crossing the foyer they had stepped into suddenly stopped and turned properly to the door. "Is this Lady Alice?" She turned her attention to Ransom for confirmation.

"It is. Lady Alice, this is my aunt Emma, Lady Wetherby."

This was Ransom's...aunt? He had brought her to the home of his aunt? Now she watched Ransom more carefully. What kind of game was he playing? This was precisely why she stuck to scientific study.

Lady Wetherby waved a hand. "Emma, please. Did you find it?" She spoke the last bit with a great deal of earnestness as she came forward and clutched Alice's hands into her own.

"I'm sorry?" Alice managed.

"The reference to the comet. Ransom mentioned you were looking for it. Do you know I thought the same thing when I read it in this month's news sheet from the Society? Have you found the reference to it yet?"

Alice looked to Ransom and back at the woman who held her hands. Ransom's aunt was likely somewhere in her sixties, but her face was remarkably unlined, her eyes gentle, and her smile fast, but that wasn't what held Alice's gaze, what kept the words stuck in her throat.

It was the woman's hair, or rather lack of it. Lady Wetherby wore her hair...short.

It fell in waves to her chin, framing her face in such a way as to make her look almost youthful. Alice could do nothing but stare until Lady Wetherby's gaze turned slightly concerned.

"I haven't found it as of yet." She glanced at Ransom. "My studies have been rather interrupted as of late, Lady Wetherby."

"Psh," she said and drew Alice's arm through hers. "And it's Emma. We'll find it. I'm sure of it."

Then Alice was being led away toward a set of doors off the foyer from which a low rumble emitted. She looked frantically at Ransom, but he lingered behind them, his gaze carefully averted. What had Emma said? Men weren't allowed? What was going on?

"Ladies!" Emma called as they reached the door. "We have a guest today. Lady Alice Atwood."

Alice's gaze swept the room, her heart ratcheting up to an impossible staccato.

The drawing room before her was filled with women.

No. No. No. No.

All of her senses seemed to erupt at once. Her instinct to be extra vigilant she had developed as a child to keep herself safe ratcheted up to intense levels.

Emma released her arm and swept into the room, greeting one woman and the next, carried away on a tide of greetings. This couldn't be happening. All these women. All of them dressed in gowns and flowery hats and white gloves and looking so perfectly normal. So perfectly at ease. So…natural.

She spun about, prepared to make a run for the door when Ransom stopped her, his hands on her shoulders. She looked up. It was impossible not to as his face was so very close to hers, and he was so very tall and…handsome.

"Alice." His voice was low and soft like it had been the previous night right before he kissed her, and the rampaging beat of her heart suddenly ceased, falling into a calm steady rhythm as she gazed into his blue, blue eyes. "Alice, I need you to trust me. This is where you belong."

She swallowed and snuck a glance behind her, but the room seemed to swell with those finely dressed ladies holding proper cups of tea and dainty plates of sandwiches and—

"Ransom, I can't." She struggled against his grip, but then he said something that left her completely motionless.

"Alice, you'll never be able to believe me if you don't first believe in yourself." He let go of her and with a dip of his head in farewell, he slipped out the door leaving her standing at the threshold of Lady Wetherby's packed drawing room.

"Blimey." Kathryn's whisper jolted Alice from her thoughts, and she turned to find the maid standing beside her. "Is this the same gent that brought you those lovely roses, my lady?" She whispered this as well even as her gaze swept the room.

Alice could only nod. Fear gripped her throat, but she didn't flee. Why didn't she flee?

Because she didn't want to disappoint Ransom.

The realization struck her directly in the chest, and pain and longing flooded through her, swamping all other emotions.

"Hello." Two women separated themselves from the crowd before them and approached, hands outstretched. They were nearly identical except for the color of their hair, one being dark and one being light. "I'm Melanie and this is my sister, May. We're the Greenawalts." It was the woman with the lighter coloring who spoke, and Alice found herself nodding before remembering to bloody well say something.

"I'm Alice." She nodded to the sister with the lighter hair. "Melanie." And then to the other. "May. Greenawalt, you said?"

The darker haired one nodded vigorously. "Oh yes, that's it."

Alice realized she was still nodding along with the sister named May, but somehow her thoughts had kept moving because suddenly she stopped for the second time in mere moments, her entire body reaching absolute stillness. She looked from one sister to the other, unable to believe her own thoughts.

"Melanie and May Greenawalt?" she said again. "As in… M.M. Greenawalt?"

Melanie's face lit at Alice's words, her smile growing ever wider. "Oh, you've read our work then?"

May pitched forward expectantly, but Alice had forgotten how to speak again. It was only sheer befuddlement at what she had discovered that kept her functioning somewhat normally.

"M.M. Greenawalt? The authors of the paper on the crystallization of geodes?" she asked.

May nodded now. "Yes, that's us. I'm flattered you've read it. It's such a niche field, you know."

Melanie gestured behind them. "Emma mentioned your interest in comets. You must come speak with Maxine Gibbons then."

"Maxine Gibbons?" Alice asked, her mind already racing ahead. "Do you mean Max Gibbons?"

"The very same," May said with a nod and a smile, gesturing behind them to a stout woman perusing a plate of petit fours.

Melanie stopped and turned back to Kathryn. "I'm sorry. I didn't get your name."

Kathryn looked to Alice in what could only be a bid for guidance, but Alice was as lost as the maid.

Kathryn shrugged and held out her hand in greeting. "The name's Kathryn. I'm Lady Alice's maid."

Melanie shook it as though she were greeting the president of the Royal Astronomical Society.

"Welcome!" she cried and pulled both of them into the room.

Within minutes Alice met not only Maxine Gibbons, whose paper on the categorization of comets had particularly peaked Alice's interest in the field, but she also met Lauren Brothers who published as Loren Brothers on the topic of deep-water discovery and the Waverly cousins who published as B and G Waverly on their discoveries in fossils on the Cornish coast. There were other women whose work was not yet published but who all seemed to know of Alice's intent on rooting out the first mention of the comet from the Scientific Scholar Society news sheet.

At some point she lost Kathryn only to find the woman across the room, teacup in one hand, petit four in the other, engaged in discussion with a woman wearing a turban.

It was amidst this confusion that Alice realized what Ransom had done. He had brought her to a room full of women scientists. The drawing room was packed with them.

Quickly her mind tried to catalog the facts. Ransom was a financial supporter of the new observatory. He said someone close to him had an interest in astronomy. Someone close to him...

Her eyes flew across the room, madly trying to locate his aunt Emma, but then—

The sound of silver against glass pinged through the room, quieting the conversation about her, and she searched for the source of the sound only to find Emma herself standing atop a chair at the front of the room. She set the glass and fork she'd been holding on the mantel behind her and clapped her hands together.

"Now then, I suppose we shall formally start this meeting of the Ladies' Scientific Guild. Evelyn, would you begin the roll call?"

A short woman with a thick braid of coarse black hair stood beside Emma on the floor, and pushing her spectacles up on her nose began to read from a journal she held open in her hands.

Alice stood where she was, rooted to the floor, her thoughts spiraling, slipping from her grasp before she could catch a single one of them.

But there was one thing she was sure of, one thing she knew above all else.

Ransom was not attempting to seduce her body. The blasted man was attempting to seduce her brain.

* * *

WHEN HE RETURNED to his aunt Emma's, he wasn't surprised when Alice launched herself into his carriage before the thing had even come to a complete stop. She yanked the door shut behind her, the slap of wood against wood ringing through the carriage.

"Explain yourself."

She was angry. He hadn't been expecting that emotion, but then he couldn't help but enjoy what it did to her.

There was color in her cheeks, a brightness to her face, that finally brought life to her person past the overpowering drab of her dress. Her hair had come slightly loose. Not so much that anyone might notice, but enough that he noticed, and it softened her features. It was a startling dichotomy. The pulsing anger on her face with the relaxed air her hair provided.

"What have I done now?" He feigned nonchalance.

She reached up and rapped on the ceiling, signaling the driver to go. He didn't know where his driver was taking them as he hadn't given the man instructions, but it didn't matter. Ransom would have responded to a knock with such fury as Alice had delivered it, and he couldn't blame the servant for responding immediately.

"You know perfectly well what you've done, and I should like an explanation."

He glanced quietly at the window as his aunt's house disappeared from view. "Would it be rude of me to interrupt your tirade to ask about the welfare of your maid?"

Alice's jaw firmed. "I gave her the rest of the day off, and I am not having a tirade."

"Quite right. I would say you're throwing one."

This had her sitting back, her mouth snapping shut.

He leaned back as well. "How was your afternoon with my aunt?"

"Informative." She shot the single word at him like a bullet.

He suppressed the grin her obvious unsettledness stoked in him. "Informative?"

She sat forward, her fingers clutching that damn reticule. "You know about your aunt's activities. About the Guild. How?"

"She tells me about it. How is it do you think I became attached to the observatory project?"

Once more her mouth snapped shut, her eyebrows popping up behind her spectacles. It was a beat before she said, "Your aunt tells you about it? You mean…she openly speaks of her interest in scientific endeavors?"

He shrugged. "Of course she does. Why wouldn't she?"

He hoped his posture of casualness would make her drop her guard when in reality he waited, braced really, for her answer. He could still see her the night before, pitched against the stone wall as if holding on to the rock itself would keep her from shattering. Something in her past had taught her to doubt herself, to believe she was somehow less. *Disappoint* was the word she had used, which suggested someone else had set expectations for her, expectations she had not met.

He ignored the familiar twist of pain in his chest and focused on the woman before him. This wasn't about him. This was about her. He just hated how much his own past seemed to be cracking the more he tried to unravel hers.

"Because it's—"

He sat forward, the silence ringing in his ears. What had she been about to say? He saw the word as it hung on her lips, but she'd stopped before speaking it.

"It's?" he prompted, but she licked her lips and looked away, and he knew the moment was lost.

When she looked back at him, her eyes were steely, her chin sure again. "How much do you know about the Guild?"

He shrugged again and leaned back, hoping to lure her out once more. "As much as I'm allowed. I'm sure you heard my aunt's rules about men being a part of the organization." Now he didn't stop a grin. "Aunt Emma can be quite formidable in protecting the sanctity of the group."

"Why no men?" Alice asked, her tone curious, which in turn made him curious.

He settled back against the bench. "Aunt Emma wished to provide a space for women to feel comfortable speaking on the subjects that most interested them. She thought male members might stifle the creativity of the group."

Her eyes remained steady on him for several seconds after he finished speaking, and he wondered what it was she was processing. But instead of speaking her thoughts, she moved, sliding over to plop on the bench beside him. She leaned close, her face suddenly earnest.

"Has your aunt ever attempted to publish any of her work?"

Her question was a departure from what they had been discussing, and it took him a moment to gather his answer. "Not to my recollection. Aunt Emma has always been more interested in supporting others in the field rather than developing her own work."

"Supporting others?"

He turned so he could face her more fully. "Aunt Emma's interest in scientific matters started with her husband. She served as his secretary the whole of their married life. It was acting in such capacity that she discovered there were other women who wished to have more of a footprint in study."

"So she started the Guild?"

He nodded. "She wanted to give them a place to safely discuss their research. She found through her work with Uncle Bart that women were reticent to step forward with their findings."

"Why?"

The force at which she spoke the word had the muscles at the back of his neck tightening. He studied her face, but it remained simply earnest, giving away no other emotion, but he couldn't help but think she wanted to ask something else.

He took her in, the tightly styled hair, the overlarge spectacles and not for the first time did he wonder if she was hiding something. Or rather, if she was hiding herself.

"I'm sure you're aware women don't particularly have the most opportunities in the world we live in."

"I am aware." This was spoken with slightly more verve.

"Aunt Emma wished to give them somewhere to safely speak." He shrugged. "It's as simple as that."

Her eyes moved over his face, and he felt his answer was suddenly inadequate. But then she asked, "What is your relationship with your aunt? You seem unusually close."

Once more he got the sense she wished to ask something else, but her question was perilously close to the thing he never spoke of, and he shifted on the bench, looking away.

"I spent holidays from school with Aunt Emma and Uncle Bart," he decided to say.

"Oh, I'm sorry," she said, backing away slightly. "I hadn't realized. Have your parents...passed?"

"Parent." The word came out more as a reaction rather than coherent thought.

Alice seemed to still beside him, but he wasn't surprised when she gave a quiet. "Oh?"

He looked out the window as if he could find a suitably vague answer there, but then he found himself turning, facing Alice directly.

"My father died when I was young. Influenza. I don't have very many memories of him, and the ones I do have aren't very clear. My mother was consumed by her grief for him and left."

"She left? She left you?" She spoke each question as though she were getting closer to the question she truly wished to ask, but what he couldn't help noticing was how she spoke the thing he had left unsaid.

His mother had left...him.

He felt the past perking up inside of him like a monster waking from a drugged sleep. He saw it stir, rumbling deep within him, and he wanted nothing more than to lull it back into submission. But he'd been doing that all his life, and now the only thing that made him feel alive was being potentially kidnapped by a bespectacled lady bent on scientific exploration. Of his person.

"She left," he decided to say. "I'm not sure she realized she was leaving me." He picked through the words even as he spoke them to see if they fit how he remembered that time. "My mother had always been the one to come to the nursery first in the morning to get me, and one morning she didn't come."

He wasn't seeing the carriage. He wasn't seeing Alice. He was seeing that day. He'd awoken in his little bed tucked in the corner of the nursery. He had made a fortress out of old blocks and books around his bed after reading a story about shipwrecked sailors, and he thought he would barricade his bed like a reinforced ship. He was so proud of it and couldn't wait to show his mother straightaway. Only not that morning. She simply didn't come.

"I waited there in my bed, watching the sun on the ceiling. It started at the window, and I watched it stretch and stretch all the way across the room, but she never came. I lay there, waiting, worried that if I were to get up and go look for her, she would be angry with me." He paused, his brow furrowing as a memory floated to the surface. "My mother was always angry with me. I remember trying to do things in a certain way to please her, but even then, when I was so young, I understood that she did things with me to please my father, but I think even when he was there, she didn't particularly wish to have anything to do with me."

Alice took his hand in hers, and it startled him from his

thoughts. It was like he was roused from sleep, and he tried to remember what he had said.

"Where did she go?"

"Catanzaro." That was an easier answer. "She and my father had visited there on their wedding trip, and she fled there upon his death. She's never returned."

"So you went to live with your aunt and uncle?" Her voice was so soft as if she feared her words might hurt him. No one had ever treated him with such care. He was Ransom Shepard, a heartless rogue and cavalier ne'er-do-well. But the way she spoke to him then it was as if he were something precious.

He felt the past roar up then, suddenly and completely he could see it all unfolding. His nanny rushing into the room hours after he'd awoken. He remembered her wide eyes, her trembling lips, her outstretched hands, but it was too late. He'd already messed the bed waiting for his mother, and the hunger in his stomach was hard and biting.

"Aunt Emma came to get me." He remembered that as well. Aunt Emma running through the door of his rooms. He didn't know when. Time was an ephemeral thing to a child. It might have been hours later, minutes, or days, he didn't know. But she had come, and he remembered. "I was so scared." He frowned, connecting the feeling with the word for the first time. He hadn't realized how scared he'd been when his mother hadn't come to wake him. But now he knew. He knew what that relief was when Aunt Emma had first picked him up, held him against her, and told him it would be all right. "Aunt Emma and Uncle Bart took me in." He shook his head and ran a hand through his hair as if shaking the past from his body. "I'm sorry. I'm not saying this right."

She squeezed his hand. He'd forgotten she had been holding it. "However you speak of it is the right way to speak of it," she said. "It's your past. You get to say whatever you wish about it."

He faced her for the first time since he'd started speaking, and he was surprised by the concern he saw on her face. More than ever, he wanted to remove her spectacles so he could better see her, as if by removing them he could see who she really was.

But more than that, right then, he wished to kiss her.

So he did. He leaned down, brushing his lips over hers, and she responded, leaning ever so slightly into him.

He had kissed many women, devoured some of them. He had done things one would never discuss in a drawing room. He had done things he wouldn't even discuss in his club. He had done everything, but he had never done this. He had never kissed a woman who meant something to him, and he pulled away, slowly, achingly slowly, as if his body didn't wish to stop kissing her, but he had to ask her something, something that suddenly burned inside of him.

When her eyes finally fluttered opened, he said, "Have you any skill at sneaking out of your home?"

She straightened, her eyes narrowing as if she were insulted by the question. "I have no need for such tactics, my lord."

He raised his eyebrows, and her expression melted into one of quiet pride.

"Why is that?" he asked.

Her quiet expression brightened to a full smile. "Because I'm a very good liar."

CHAPTER 8

"*W*hat did you tell your uncle?"

"I told him I was going to the library."

"At this hour?" He looked about them at the deserted streets, the soft glow of the lamps. A carriage disappeared at the cross street, so far away from them it was as though it were a phantom. "It's nearly midnight. Libraries aren't open."

"Yes, but Uncle Herman doesn't realize that. I gave him Westinghouse's treatise on the principles of voltaic stacks. He won't even know what day of the week it is until it's already next week."

"You are a good liar."

She held up a finger. "Preparedness. Good lying requires a great deal of preparation."

He snatched the hand she held up and drew it through his arm, propelling her in the direction of the next block.

"Where exactly are you taking me now?" She wasn't at all anticipating the Guild, and she wondered what other measures he held up his sleeve. "I must say I didn't realize seduction required quite so much walking."

"I didn't wish for my carriage to be recognized." He

looked up and down the street they reached for only a second before bustling her along.

He only held her arm, but a jolt of pleasure rushed through her at the way he took charge, navigating them through the dark streets of Mayfair.

He glanced at her, and she worried she'd been quiet for too long. She wasn't sure why it was she became so talkative in his presence, but there was something about him that simply drew her out. It was as though over twenty years of controlled silence had burst like a failed dam when there was suddenly someone with whom she could speak without risking criticism or outright rejection.

She didn't know when it was that she had begun to trust him like that, but she had a suspicion it was well before his revelation in the carriage after the Guild meeting. What he had told her about his mother only served to shatter the last of the mystique that surrounded him as London's most notorious rogue.

"You have your knife in that reticule, don't you? I shouldn't like to be out here without knowing you are armed."

She raised her chin. "Of course I have my knife. Should you like to see it?" She moved to open her reticule, but he shook his head.

"No, that's quite all right. Simply knowing you have it is enough." He smiled playfully but even though he joked with her, his smile still sent a zing of anticipation through her.

The Guild meeting had been one thing, but this was something entirely different. Would he finally seduce her? They were after all scurrying through the cover of darkness like two fugitives bent on something upon which polite society would frown. It surely must be something important, especially if he didn't wish for someone to spot his carriage.

She hadn't expected seduction lessons to be quite this...

stealthy. For a moment, panic gripped her that perhaps the letter writer was right. Was there something so unnatural about her that London's most notorious rogue couldn't conduct a seduction using his normal methods? Or *were* these his normal methods?

She looked about them at the empty streets, the dark night surrounding them, and wondered how much she didn't truly know. The street they were now on contained homes separated by long stretches of garden walls, and she wondered what kind of wealth could obtain so much greenery in such a congested part of town. Ransom was an earl but surely…

Taking her hand in his, Ransom turned abruptly, slipping them down the alley between two walled gardens. Her heart thundered at the sudden shadows, the way he seemed to move in so little light, his footsteps sure, his grip on her hand secure.

It was darker here than on the street, and she could hardly discern where he was taking her. He stopped abruptly in front of an iron door, the details of which were lost in the shadows.

He dropped her hand to come up on his toes, reaching to the carved limestone above the door. There was a scraping noise, and he dropped back to the balls of his feet. There was a different scraping noise now, one that rang with the sound of metal, and the door opened. He must have retrieved a key from somewhere.

She stilled even as he slipped through the door. "Ransom," she whispered, although there couldn't possibly be anyone about to overhear. "Are we trespassing?"

Instead of answering, he extended a hand to her through the open door, and a shaft of moonlight lit his mischievous smile. "It's not trespassing if you own the property."

Her breath caught in her lungs as realization settled in her stomach with the heaviness of anticipation.

Ransom had brought her to his home.

He stood before her, hand outstretched, and she suddenly knew that she was the only woman he'd ever done this with. She didn't know how she could be so certain, but there was something in it. Perhaps it was the way the night fell on her shoulders or the way the moon seemed to catch only his smile. But this moment marked a change in whatever it was between them. There would be a before now and there would be an after, and she very much feared the end of the after.

For the end would come. That was what she knew of things like this. They always ended.

But she took his hand anyway and let him lead her into the dark garden beyond because even though it may end, she would always have these moments, with him, to remember, to look back on, to hold against her heart when the alternative was having nothing at all.

She didn't know what might have caused this shift, this change that seemed to have overcome him. He'd been so reluctant that first night in the carriage, denying her request outright. But now...now he was leading her through the darkness, wishing to show her something, and his words from that day in his aunt's foyer came back to her.

Why would he care if she believed in herself? He could have easily seduced her by now. She had thought she had made it more than obvious that she was willing, and yet he hadn't done it. He hadn't done more than touch her ever so much, and it was nothing by which one would have said she was ruined. She had come upon debutantes and dandies doing far more in dark corners in her limited experience with society.

Instead he prolonged it as though he were looking for

something. Something in her, and she worried he might not find it.

Then why bring her here? To his home?

The path they traveled was comprised of flat stones, and she was glad she had worn her walking shoes. Slippers would have been deadly on this uneven ground in the dark, and her heart picked up pace, her muscles flooding with an exhilaration she had only ever felt before when picking up a book.

Was this what it was like? This thrill that shot through her when he touched her? The sense of floating that seemed to encapsulate her when she was near him? Was this what drove people to do irrational things? Was this what made her sister marry a man who didn't love her in return?

Things that had once seemed murky started to come together then, there in the dark in the Earl of Knighton's garden, and she wondered what else she had missed. She felt a pang of loss but only briefly, the passage of time blunting its effect.

Hedges rose up on either side of them, and she couldn't see much but the few feet in front of them, and then without warning, Ransom plunged them into a thicket of trees. He pushed aside branches, leading her through what she realized was a worn path in the dirt at her feet, the ground clear beneath her shoes.

He pushed through a screen of branches, popping them free into a small clearing and there was…a boat.

She darted her gaze between the boat and Ransom. Slowly she became aware of water, a small pond stretching out in front of them. The light was better here clear of the thicket of trees, and she vaguely made out its shape. It was some kind of water folly set deep in the gardens. She looked around, but there were no other structures near it.

He gestured to the boat with a charming flourish. "My lady, may I help you board?"

She looked again at the boat, this time noting its contents. It was some kind of small, wooden skiff, but the center seat had been removed and in its place were—

Oh God, the boat was filled with cushions and quilts, pillows stacked against one end like the head of a bed.

Heat curled in her stomach, and she almost pressed a hand to it, hoping to still the sudden tumult of—was that desire?

Her eyes flashed to his, but he was only grinning, his hand remaining outstretched. The heat was replaced by something deeper, more complex. When he looked at her like that, there was a sense of place, something she had never felt before. It was almost as if he wished her to be there, with him. No one had ever wanted her to be with them.

"Thank you, kind sir," she said just as grandly and took his hand as he helped her into the boat.

She reclined against the pillows as the cushioned bottom was not receptive to sitting up. There was some jostling as Ransom pushed the boat from the shoreline, and he adeptly jumped in as the skiff floated away from the shore. There was a single oar in the boat, tucked along one side and he knelt, slipping it free to dip into the water.

She pressed her hands against the cushion along her back, the boat rocking gently, water sloshing along its sides. The earthy dampness of the pond invaded her senses then as they neared the center of the pond, far away from the overpowering scents of the garden, and it was somehow soothing. She relaxed, her fingers going weak against the cushion.

Ransom paddled only a few times before stowing the oar once more. She held her breath. She couldn't help it. This was what she had been waiting for. The moment when she would discover if the letter writer had been right. If all of them had been right.

Except he didn't touch her. He dropped to the cushion

beside her, nestling his head into the bank of pillows at her side, and then he stared resolutely at—

The sky.

She blinked once or twice, her heart hammering in her chest. What was he doing? Why hadn't he—

"If you stare at me all night, you'll miss the point of all of this."

She swung her gaze away, embarrassment hot and piercing. When her vision finally cleared, she traced the outline of the trees hanging over the water, their branches full and heavy, hazy shapes in the near darkness. Somewhere there was a rustling, soft and fading, and she pictured a nocturnal animal scurrying about for its dinner.

She drew a deep breath, pushing down her rioting emotions, and looked directly upward.

And the air froze in her lungs, her fingers curling instinctively into the cushion at her back, her eyes wide and unblinking.

"Ransom," she whispered, the only thing she was able to say.

"I thought you might like it." His words were equally as quiet, and then he slipped his hand into hers. That was all. His body lay next to hers, pressed fully to her side, and she could feel the heat of him through layers of clothes. But all he did was take her hand.

Because the true gift he had given her was above them. A carpet of stars unfurling in the black sky. It was like her own personal galaxy had been unrolled just for her. Her eyes swam, drinking in the sight of it. Her gaze darted from constellation to constellation, and she knew their names or at least she had only minutes ago, but just then, lying there with the soft rocking of the boat hypnotizing her, the faint echo of a night breeze reaching her ears, the smaller sound of their breathing, slow and deep, it served to transfix her, and she couldn't think of anything at all.

Except maybe how he held her hand. That she felt more than understood. He cradled it, his fingers laced so carefully through hers as though he wished to hold on to her but didn't want to make her feel trapped.

"Ransom, it's beautiful."

He didn't say anything at first, and she wished to look at him, the need to see his face stronger than the allure of the stars. She turned her head and was surprised to find his profile hard, as if her statement had confused him.

But then he spoke. "I like to come out here to think." His voice even held a note of confusion, and she wasn't sure if it was because she had suddenly dominated his nights, and instead of finding himself in the throes of passion with a beautiful woman, he was lying in a boat staring at the sky...with her.

But she didn't think that was it. Because in his voice she heard something familiar. The curious tone of someone speaking who had not spoken of such personal things before, who may, like her, have never had someone in whom one could confide.

"I used to think about my father a great deal. I don't remember him, and sometimes I wonder what he would have wanted for me. Both as a man and as an earl." He shook his head, a small back and forth against the cushions. "But I'll never know. The only person who knew who he truly was, was my mother, and unless she returns, I won't ever know."

Her heart pinched at the longing in his voice, and she squeezed his hand. "What do you think about now?" She kept her tone low, afraid to spook him.

His lips parted, but he seemed to change his mind, his mouth curving into a thoughtful smile as if he had surprised himself.

Then he turned his head and said, "Lately, I've been mostly thinking about you."

* * *

IT WASN'T REAL. She had to remind herself of that, but when he spoke those words, when his voice was deep and rich and full, when he looked at her like that—she wished it were real. She wished all of it were real.

A pain like she had never felt before unraveled in her stomach. She had been so focused on proving the letter writer wrong she hadn't considered how she would feel in this. The emotions it would invoke, the wants she didn't know she had. The desire she couldn't have imagined.

She swallowed, feeling the enormity of what was happening fall around her like a suffocating cloak. "You... do?" She struggled to keep her voice steady, but she couldn't let him know how much he affected her just then. He would think she was weak, letting herself dream of things that would never happen.

This was an arrangement, and she had to remember that.

"I do." His voice was fuller now, a hint of playfulness returning to it. "Do you know what I think about?"

She thought she said no, but then he came up on his elbow, released her hand to lean over her, and she forgot the rudiments of speech. He was so big, his shoulders blocking out the stars above, and a rush of sheer anticipation coursed through her.

She wanted him to touch her. The need was sudden and penetrating, and she marveled at its swiftness. She'd never felt anything like it before, and surely that was a sign her experiment was working.

As soon as the thought entered her mind though, she pushed it away.

She didn't want to think of this as an experiment. She wanted to believe that Ransom was here of his own free will, that he wanted her, that he truly desired her. It was a farce, and she knew that, but just this once she wanted to believe.

He reached up with one hand and traced the line of her jaw with a single finger, heat burning through her at his touch. "I think about…" His voice trailed off as his finger lazily made its way to her chin and down along the sensitive curve of her neck, along her collarbone. And then it stopped, and his eyes met hers. "I think about what you look like behind those spectacles."

Before she could understand what he had said, he reached up and tugged her spectacles from her face, his grin like that of a curious child, but as soon as they came free, the grin vanished. The moment froze in time, him leaning above her, her spectacles in his hand, her arms reaching up, grasping his shoulders in a nervous reaction to stop him from taking her lenses.

And the look on his face.

God, the look on his face cut right through her.

Disbelief. Shock. Confusion.

She wanted more than anything to know what he was thinking. What he saw when he looked at her without the shield of her spectacles. Could he even see her in the dark?

He reached out that single finger again, but this time he touched her cheek, traced a path to her temple.

"Beautiful." He whispered the single word, sincerity making his voice breathless, and for a moment, she actually believed him. Then he shook his head and said, "You shouldn't be hiding behind these. Do you really need them to see?"

And then the worst thing happened. He sat up, holding the spectacles up to his eyes as if to peer through them.

"No." The word came out much too loudly, splitting the

tranquil night, and she rushed to sit up, rocking the boat wildly, water sloshing madly at its sides as she scrambled to stop him, but it was too late. Her hands hung futilely in front of her as she made to reach for her spectacles, but he was already peering through him.

She waited, her heart thundering in her chest, her mind racing with the accusations she knew were coming, but he didn't speak. He only lowered the spectacles to his lap, his gaze drifting to her face.

"You don't need these," he finally said. "They're nothing but glass."

No accusation. No condemnation. Only quiet understanding. Still her heart pounded. But what she heard in his voice was something else she hadn't expected. There was no surprise this time. It was as though he had already suspected her of the ruse.

"Why do you wear these, Alice?" Only a question, a question she wished to answer for the first time in her life.

But she couldn't look at him. She dropped her gaze to her hands, fiddling with her skirts as she said, "I found it was easier when I wore them. People tend not to see those who are different from them, and the spectacles were an easy way to—" The words suddenly clogged in her throat. She'd never said this before, not even to her own sisters, and she found it was difficult to put into words what she simply understood. She gripped her skirts in her hands and raised her chin, meeting his gaze directly. "I got tired of her yelling at me, of always criticizing me. When I put on the spectacles, it got quiet. It was like she'd given up. The spectacles were a step too far and even she couldn't save me." The unfortunate wallflower that was Alice, the plain, terribly intelligent and bookish Alice. The daughter who wasn't a lady and wasn't a son.

She didn't say that part because she didn't want Ransom

to think of her that way. Think of her as something unsavory and unwanted. She liked believing he *could* want her.

"Who was criticizing you, Alice?"

Why did he keep saying her name like that? Why did he have to keep her pinned to this conversation with nothing more than his voice?

She swallowed. "My mother. My mother did the criticizing, and my father did the avoiding." She plucked at her skirts, the fight drained out of her. "May I have them back now?"

He didn't give them to her. Instead he folded them closed and tucked them into the pocket of his jacket.

Then he cupped her face in both of his hands and kissed her.

She thought by now she would be used to it. She could anticipate his kiss, know the feel of his lips against hers, the way his touch made her heart stampede and her body flush. But she'd never get used to this, not even if she had the rest of her life to kiss him.

It wasn't just the physical part of the kiss. It was everything else. His kiss had the power to make the rest of it vanish. The echoes of her mother's disdain, or her father's rejection. The shadows that swirled about her, their greedy hands reaching for her, wanting to pull her down into their dark depths. It all went away, and suddenly she was Alice, perfectly normal and perfectly lovable Alice.

She wanted that. She wanted that blissful peace more than anything, and she reached up, wrapping her arms around him as he laid her back against the cushions.

He didn't break the kiss, his lips searing into hers, and she felt the pulse of desire begin to simmer low in her belly. Would he finally do it? Would he touch her in all of the places she longed to be touched? Places she wasn't even aware of before he'd first kissed her.

He traced his lips over her cheeks and temples much as he had done with that single wandering finger, and she curled her hands into his shoulders, arching her neck to get even closer to him. But he shifted, his lips going to her neck as if he sensed her opening to him. Heat. Heat pressed against her neck, and a shiver ran through her, her hands clutching now, the desire growing painfully sharp within her.

"Ransom." His name got lost on the night breeze, but it needn't matter.

His hands were moving, following the dips and curves of her torso, her hips. When his hand skimmed the side of her breast, she jerked, surprised by the flash of longing it ignited inside of her.

He paused, his hand and lips stilling in their sensual assault.

"You like that," he murmured against her skin.

She only managed a garbled murmur of affirmation. His lips were already moving again, dipping lower along her collarbone as his hand shifted, skimming just below her breast. She arched, this time pressing her chest into him, trying to get closer to his touch.

She felt his smile against her now. "Is there something you'd like, Alice?" He leaned above her now, his face an outline against the starry sky. "Tell me what you want." The hand that had been against her breast stroked her cheek.

"I feel…" she began, but she didn't know the right words. She took the hand at the side of her face and brought it back to her breast, but she wasn't brave enough to place his palm against her. She simply held it in her hand. "I want you to touch me…here."

He disappeared again, his head bending once more to the task of kissing her, his lips retracing their route to her neck, her collarbone…lower. His hand skimmed the underside of her breast again before slipping higher, his fingers playing with the edge of her bodice. His mouth had made its way to her shoulder then, and then…and then…

Her sleeve slipped over the crest of her shoulder, her bodice loosening the smallest of degrees, but it was as though he had stripped her bare. His wandering fingers plucked at the edge of her bodice, pushing the fabric aside, and—

Oh God, he slipped his hand beneath her gown, his callused fingertips coursing fiery paths across her chest, lower, until—

"Ransom." She jerked as his hand closed over her straining nipple. He stilled, but he didn't pull back.

"Alice." His tone held a note of question, and she knew he would stop if only she asked, but she didn't want him to stop. She wanted more. She wanted all of it.

This time she arched into his hand, inviting him to touch her without saying a word. His hand moved again, circling her nipple with a ring of heat. Her hands went back to his shoulders, grasping, trying to hold on as his mouth ravaged her neck, the sensitive spot behind her ear.

But then his hand was gone.

"Ransom." Was that her voice? So whiny and begging?

He was adjusting her, slipping her other sleeve from her shoulder, pushing her bodice down until—

The cool night air struck her nipples, and they tightened convulsively. She was bared to him, and she wanted to close her eyes against the vulnerability, but she couldn't. She had to see his face.

He leaned above her. She thought he might drink her in, the sight of her lying bared beneath him, but his eyes were on her face, studying her with a curious attention.

"You are beautiful." His voice was thick, and she couldn't help but think his words were an answer to a question he had only asked of himself.

He shifted over her, and when his mouth returned to her

skin, she felt the hunger in him now as he ravaged her breasts, first one and then the other, with his kisses. She writhed, her legs caught in her skirts even as she tried to wrap them around him, hold him closer as he made the desire in her twist to a painful knot.

As if sensing her distress, his hand traveled to her leg, inched up her skirts by a fistful of fabric at a time. She felt the rush of night air against the exposed skin at the top of her stockings, and finally, she let her legs fall to the side, opening herself to him. His fingers moved quickly, following the curve of her knee, discovering the edge of her stocking, skating higher.

Oh God, was he going to…would he touch her…there?

He *did*.

"Ransom." She spasmed at his touch, coming up off the cushion at her back, her most intimate part pressing into the palm of his hand.

But he didn't stop his advance. His fingers toyed with her folds, and she could feel a sudden dampness there as though her body wept for him. He sucked her nipple into his mouth at the moment he touched her sensitive nub, and the feeling was too much. She cried out, her fingers digging into his shoulders, passion roaring through her.

He didn't stop, his finger circling her nub, gently, softly, coaxing her toward…something. She could feel it, the way he so carefully brought her body to the brink only to stop, his fingers stilling against her. She could feel nothing but the parts of her where he touched her as though her senses could only focus on that, on what he was doing to her, and nothing more.

His fingers began to move again, the circles ever tightening, and she knew something was just out of reach. No, that wasn't it. He was keeping it at bay. So skillful and wicked was his touch that he could keep her there, play with her, stoke her desires.

And it was too much. The realization of what he was doing, the power his teasing held over her, and she shattered, the climax taking over every last bit of her.

It shook her, the power of her orgasm, and it was several moments before she realized how tightly she had closed her eyes, so caught up in her own passion that she hadn't realized she'd even done it. But then her eyes fluttered open, and she saw the stars above her, heard the soft rustle of the night breeze in the trees around them, and the gentle sway of the boat on the water.

Ransom had pulled her bodice back into place, and she lay nestled in his arms. He held her even as her body still hummed from the climax he'd given her. She wanted to stay there forever, in the quiet of the night, in the harbor of his arms, in this moment where for once she felt normal.

She felt peace.

But she knew even as she pressed her face into his chest, felt the beat of his heart against her cheek, she knew it wasn't real and at some point, she would be forced to wake up from this dream.

CHAPTER 9

*H*e decided to walk to his club.

It was not an easy walk. In fact, it was a few miles, but he thought the exercise might clear his head. It had rained that morning, and the pavement was littered with wet patches that added to his mental distraction as he worked to avoid them. The sun was already well up in the sky, however, and he knew the puddles would be gone before long.

This was what he was thinking about—puddles, for God's sake—in order to avoid thinking about the very real thing that had happened.

He had brought Alice home.

While he had not brought her inside the house, he had still brought her to his residence. No one had seen them, he had made sure of that, so there was no danger to her reputation. But it was rather the damage to himself he feared.

He was letting her in.

He hadn't meant to do it, but he had. Little by little, she was pulling things out of him that he hadn't been willing to reveal to himself. Not in a very long time. The crusty exterior he had built around himself was falling away like a snake would shed its skin, and he hated it.

When this nonsense about seduction lessons was over, he would go back to the life he had worked so hard to establish. The careless rogue, the ne'er-do-well rake. It was safer that way.

Then why did he keep bringing her closer?

When he'd removed her spectacles, the sight of her face had stopped his heart. He had been right. She was hiding behind those damn things. Only the reasons why were far worse than he had imagined.

Far worse because he could feel exactly how she felt. Yearning for the unconditional love one's mother was to provide and instead finding harshness and rejection. Or in his case, having that love simply disappear one morning, leaving him untethered from the father he never knew.

He walked with his hands tucked firmly in his pockets, his head down, his boots scraping along the pavement. He was in no rush, and he hoped the longer he spent ruminating along his walk the clearer his mind would be when he arrived at his club.

To drink himself into oblivion should the walk not work.

This was preposterous. He had meetings that afternoon. The observatory at College Park was due to open in a fortnight, and there was an investors meeting with Lord Dalton that afternoon to discuss the opening night gala. He was to meet with his solicitors beforehand to discuss the purchase of a parcel to expand his Yorkshire estate, and then there was—

Alice.

He scrubbed a hand over his face, growling into his palm, which earned concerned glances from a pair of ladies he happened to be passing at the time. He dipped his hat in their direction and tried to smile reassuringly, but he feared it came out as more of a grimace.

Aunt Emma had been right. He shouldn't have dallied with Lady Alice Atwood. She was far too good for him. Perhaps that was why she had invaded his thoughts.

Except he knew it wasn't that. It was the fact that in her he saw himself. For the first time, he could see the part of himself he hid from everyone reflected back at him, and suddenly he wasn't quite so alone.

He started walking faster.

That was it. He simply had to get his heart rate up, and his thoughts would clear. He could focus on the day ahead and attend to his business matters with the focus they deserved.

He rounded the last corner that would bring him to his club much sooner than he would have expected, and he wondered just how quickly he had been walking. He felt a light sheen of perspiration as the day grew humid, but his mind was no better for the exercise.

Drink it was then.

Only he never made it into his club.

As soon as he turned the corner, the men were on him. Three of them to be exact, all strangers to him but he knew the type. Dandies all of them with peach cravats and paisley waistcoats, their pressed trousers disappearing into shoes that far too closely resembled a lady's slippers. But the dangerous thing about dandies was they believed themselves greater than they were.

So he was not surprised when the biggest of the three pushed him. Like a bully in a schoolyard no less. He wished he could blame Alice for his distracted thoughts, but he wouldn't be so unfair as to think such a thing, so as he was falling backward, tucking in his arms to prevent an accidental break, he thought seriously about the steps he had taken that had brought him to that moment.

Because he had a very real uneasiness about why a gentleman had just pushed him in the street in front of his club.

He landed with a thud, and as his luck would have it, he landed directly in a puddle, soupy with mud. The splash erupted around him, soaking his jacket and hat, and he could feel the mud laboriously oozing down his cheeks. He didn't bother standing. He sat in the puddle and propped his arms on his bent knees. He peered up at his bully from his position in the mud.

"I take it you're an acquaintance of Lord Ridgeway," he said.

The dandy who had pushed him had been gesturing proudly to his friends, and at Ransom's words, he froze, his cocky smile tipping into a frown.

"That's right," he said, his accent clearly honed at Eton. "And I'm here to tell you you'd best be readying your seconds. Ridgeway will not be cuckolded."

The other two gentlemen were nodding along as if to affirm their friend's statement.

"Except he's already been cuckolded," Ransom pointed out.

This earned him a trio of confused glares.

"He won't be cuckolded...anymore!" said the second tallest dandy.

Ransom sighed. "I have received the message, gentlemen. Was there anything further you wished to add?"

He didn't really care what these gentlemen had to say. He was truly finding the entire ordeal rather annoying. He almost hoped Ridgeway would return soon to get the whole bloody thing over with.

There were other matters that demanded his attention. Ones with soft brown eyes and timid smiles. And if he closed his eyes, he could picture her, arms akimbo, demanding answers or clutching a pitcher she'd used to douse him with in an attempt at kidnapping.

Lord Ridgeway was nothing more than a pest.

Still. The dandies loomed over him, exchanging awkward glances. He sighed and finally pushed to his feet, mud and rainwater sloshing off of him. He made a couple of half-hearted attempts to brush the dust from the still dry portions of his trousers, but it was useless.

Eventually the gentleman who had pushed him raised his chin on a nod. "There's nothing else to add. Old Ridgeway will take care of the rest when he arrives." He snickered at this as if finding the situation amusing.

Ransom couldn't bring himself to care. A drink at his club was obviously out of the question now. He would be required to go home and bath before his afternoon of meetings, and he found the entire situation more inconvenient than anything. This Ridgeway bloke couldn't return to London fast enough as far as he was concerned.

"You'd better get your jollies in with that Atwood girl while you can. Although if your reputation is half true, I can't see why you'd wish to have your last plow be with a dog like her."

The dandy was still guffawing when Ransom punched him. The man's head snapped back before his body contorted, pitching backward into the clumsy arms of his mates.

Rubbing the abused knuckles of his right hand, Ransom leaned forward. "You're lucky your mate Ridgeway has already taken up my time with a duel or I would be forced to call you out. As it is, it's probably wise I never hear you speak Lady Alice Atwood's name again."

The man clutched at his nose, blood seeping through his fingers as his friends tried to tip him back onto his feet. They muttered words of apology, even the two who had said hardly a word through the whole exchange, bundling their friend off in the direction of the club, leaving Ransom standing on the sidewalk, mud dripping from his coat.

He massaged his hand before raising it to summon a hackney. He had whiskey at home. Lots of it.

* * *

SHE WAS NOT PAYING ATTENTION.

This was rather new for her. Alice couldn't help but be observant. It not only came from her studies, but it was a rather advantageous side effect of being ignored.

But that day in Lady Wetherby's drawing room, Alice Atwood was not paying the least attention.

Her thoughts were on Ransom.

She shifted in her seat, the tea in her forgotten cup sloshing ever so slightly as she did so.

Perhaps her thoughts weren't directly on Ransom but rather what they had done together.

She should be thinking about the letter writer, about his damning accusations. *Unnatural.* But it was almost funny how little she thought of the letter writer now. What had been her goal in this endeavor suddenly seemed insignificant, almost childish. What did the letter writer know of her anyway?

And more importantly, what was she going to do once she had reached her conclusions from this experiment? Was she going to write him back?

She scratched absently at her forehead, worrying over her own question. How had she not considered this aspect of her plan? It was likely the overwhelming need to prove the writer wrong that had catapulted her into action rather than thinking through all the steps. That was something terribly unlike her, and she didn't care to think of it.

However, she was coming to understand her plan in theory was not at all what it had turned out to be in truth. While she had thought her experiment wouldn't involve emotions at all, she found they were a great deal messier than she had anticipated and refused to be contained. She was even beginning to think an experiment that may involve them was perhaps not the most scientific endeavor.

She shifted again, the tea sloshing even more now as she thought about her own feelings. Heat flashed through her just thinking about what they had done, but it was soon replaced by a calming sense of ease. What she and Ransom had done that night on the little boat under the stars should have seemed scandalous, but it didn't feel that way to her at all. If anything, it seemed inevitable.

Almost…natural.

This had her sitting up, the tea sloshing violently enough that she set the teacup aside on the small table at her elbow.

Was it finished then? Had she done enough to prove the letter writer wrong? But then, how could such evidence as *emotions* be empirical enough for scientific study? It was only her word on which to found her conclusions.

A sensation she could only relate to swiftness swept through her as her thoughts continued to stampede through her mind. Was this it? Was this the result she had been seeking when she had asked Ransom to seduce her? Was this…enough?

But if it were enough, it would mean her experiments were over. She was not so unschooled as to understand he had not ruined her. Not entirely.

Not…yet.

She bit her lip, her thoughts almost too much to contain, and physical action was required to keep them from spilling into the room and into the middle of the meeting of the Ladies' Scientific Guild.

She glanced around at the other members then. They all sat with such rapt attention, focused on the speaker at that moment, a Lady Trenholm who was speaking of her latest research into the field of magnets. Some of the ladies gathered sat with hands clenched around teacups while others nibbled on shortbread, but all sat focused on Lady Trenholm. How could they not hear Alice's thoughts? How could they not see her squirm from her internal dialogue?

It was so unusual for her to have such a scandalous secret. Well, if not scandalous at least slightly improper. She was used to having secrets society would have frowned upon, but this was something different entirely. This was something more precious because it only existed between her and Ransom. It was no one else's to discover.

And if that was the case, she had returned to her initial problem. How was she to prove the letter writer wrong?

Perhaps if she knew who the man was, she could confront him. Prove that she…trembled when Ransom so much as spoke her name?

Oh God, this was never going to work.

She couldn't very well tell Ransom what she had just realized. He would have no reason to remain engaged in their arrangement, and she—

She didn't want it to end.

She swallowed and reached for her teacup. Taking a long swallow of now cold tea, she willed the shaking in her hands to cease. How had she let *this* happen? At the start of all of this, that night in his carriage when she had attempted to kidnap him, she hadn't thought this was even possible. That she would come to care for Ransom, that she may even…love him.

She swallowed the rest of the tea and discarded the cup with a not indelicate clatter.

Was this what love was? This mess of conflicting

emotions that tumbled through a person without notice? How outrageously untidy. And not in the least convenient.

The meeting had moved on, and Lady Wetherby spoke now, standing to address the gathering.

Clenching her hands in her skirt, Alice forced herself to pay attention. Lady Wetherby had been kind enough to extend an invitation to Alice directly to attend this meeting, and Alice could not show such disrespect as to not pay attention to the proceedings.

"The opening night of the observatory. Have any of you made your plans to attend?" Lady Wetherby asked.

Alice looked about. She hadn't realized the opening night of the observatory was to be a public event. These sorts of things were usually by invitation only. She wondered if Ransom had something to do with it.

A small woman behind Alice raised a hand, and Alice tried to remember the woman's name. Mrs. Harrison, perhaps?

"I for one will be there. If anyone else would like to arrive with me, I should be happy to have my driver pick you up on the way."

There was a murmur of appreciation for this offer before another hand came up on the opposite side of the room. This was from one of the Ms. Greenawalts.

"I will most certainly be there. I shouldn't miss the opportunity," May said.

"Especially as it may be one of the only chances for us to see it," her sister said with a derisive snort.

This comment was followed by a rumble of agitated agreement. Alice looked around, a feeling of sudden disagreement unspooling through the gathering.

Not one to be left confused, Alice raised her hand and said, "What do you mean by that? It was my understanding the new observatory was to be open to members of the public who wish to engage in study there."

From what she had read of the new facility there was to be a membership to be sure, but taking in the dress and stature of the women who made up the Guild, Alice didn't think any would be unable to pay the membership fees. But at her comment, there was a swift and uneasy response, heads shaking in the negative and harsh whispers cast between the members.

Lady Wetherby raised a hand as if to restore order. "Oh, I quite forgot, Lady Alice. I do beg your pardon. You've only just joined us, and we've already discussed the limitations of the new observatory." Lady Wetherby clasped her hands together. "Perhaps we should review the operational details of the observatory."

"I'd be happy to do so," Melanie Greenawalt said as she stood. "The new observatory is open to *male* membership only. Women will be granted access between the hours of nine and eleven every third Wednesday of the month." She pinched her lips into a thin, aggressive line before perfunctorily resuming her seat.

Incredulity swept through Alice first. "But the literature doesn't specify that it is to be restricted to male members?"

Lady Wetherby folded her hands across her stomach, a severe frown on her face. "I'm aware. I have addressed this with a certain member of the investors." She said this with a knowing tilt of her head, and Alice felt a small wave of discomfort, her gaze sweeping to the others to see if they had noticed the hidden message in Lady Wetherby's words. "I thought it should be made more noticeable when the pamphlets about its construction were distributed."

"So it's true then?" Alice looked from Lady Wetherby to the other members, her eyes taking in the sea of nodding heads.

"I'm afraid so," Lady Wetherby confirmed, her frown morphing into an expression of compassion, her lips screwed up to one side.

Alice stood, unable to keep her seat a moment longer. "But that's...unfair." She nearly spat the word.

It seemed so inadequate for the roil of emotions she felt just then, and ridiculously, she wanted to blame the letter writer, but she knew the letter writer was only the manifestation of the resistance she'd felt all along. The pushback she found at every turn when she had tried to step too far into scientific study, a field dominated by men.

Men who kept trying to push her out, push her down...reject her.

With sudden stark clarity, she realized she was furious. The strength of the emotion tore through her, shaking her arms and legs, so she had to clutch at her skirts to keep upright, to keep still, to prevent herself from running from the room.

But wait. Wasn't that the answer?

"Unfair is a rather more delicate word than I would use," Melanie Greenawalt murmured.

"Aye," her sister said. "We respect your restraint."

Lady Wetherby's eyes narrowed, a line of concern appearing between her brows. "I've tried speaking to the investors, but—"

"They wouldn't listen," Alice interrupted because she already knew. She had experienced it herself. No one ever seemed to *listen*.

Lady Wetherby only shook her head.

The fury inside of Alice solidified then, her limbs falling slack, the tension unwinding. It was as though for the first time she realized who she was seeing just then. Lady Wetherby was the woman who had rescued Ransom the day his mother had disappeared. She was the one who had taken him in, taken care of him, raised him. She likely loved him like a mother would, held him precious and dear.

While Alice was coming to fear she might be in love with the man, she had no such reservations about him. Part of her was still disappointed her kidnapping scheme hadn't been quite as successful as she had wished.

She raised her chin. "He might not have listened to you, but he will listen to me," she said and marched from the room, oblivious to the amused grin Lady Wetherby tried to hide.

CHAPTER 10

*H*is bath water had grown cold several minutes earlier, but he made no attempt to get out of it. He pressed the tumbler of whiskey he'd poured from the bottle on the stool at his elbow to his forehead and closed his eyes, pondering how on earth his life had gotten quite so messy. He opened his eyes long enough to take in the crumpled pile of his clothes, stiff with dried mud now, on the opposite side of the room, and almost laughed at how literal his thoughts were.

Almost. Laughed.

He took a swallow of the whiskey and replaced the glass against his forehead.

This business with Lord Ridgeway was a damn nuisance. It wasn't as though this was his first run-in with an upset husband, but they were usually far tamer. Who the bloody hell did this Lord Ridgeway think he was? Ransom had never heard a whisper about the man. Not in his clubs, not in Parliament, not even in ballrooms. So why had he taken a keen interest in getting his revenge?

And why did the man feel the need for such vengeance? He lived in Pairs with *his mistress*.

People were damn confusing.

Alice included.

He leaned back in the tub, resting his back against the copper and letting his arms drop to the sides. Cold water shifted noisily around his hips, but he ignored it. There was no need to get out, and quite frankly, he wasn't eager to face the outside world so soon after his encounter with Lord Ridgeway's bullies. He had sent the kitchen boy out with notes canceling his afternoon obligations. He wasn't leaving the house until he had figured out at least one of his problems, and as he had no knowledge of Lord Ridgeway's travel plans, he decided Alice was the only problem to be worked out and when it came to her, there was only one solution.

He was going to marry her.

There was no other way around it. The idea had come to him, completely formed and resolute, the moment his fist had struck the face of Ridgeway's bully earlier that morning. The title would require him to wed at some point. He had pushed off the deed as long as possible, uninterested in a society marriage. Uninterested in marriage at all. But if he had to see the deed done, he wouldn't do it with anyone else.

He liked Alice, genuinely, and he couldn't remember liking someone quite so much since he had met Ash at school.

He liked talking to Alice. Hell, he liked being in her company. He felt…safe with her.

His eyes drifted to the desk under the window. Her spectacles lay there, illuminated by a puddle of sunlight that had filtered through the crack in the drapes behind it. She had worn spectacles she didn't need like a shield against a mother who not only didn't love her but found her less than. If anyone could possibly understand how he felt about his past, it would be Alice.

Why not marry her? Why not have a partner who understood his limitations? Someone who would not threaten his careful defenses?

It was all perfectly reasonable, and yet he sat there in a cold bath, unwilling to move.

Because a horrible little part of him wanted Alice to be loved, and he wanted to be the one to love her.

That was the other realization that had come to him when he'd punched Lord Ridgeway's bully.

That night in the boat had shifted everything. It was all the same. His life, his future, his ideas about that future, but it was somehow just one degree off since the moment he had slipped her spectacles from her face.

He scrubbed his free hand over his face. Alice deserved to be loved, but even thinking of the word had his stomach tightening.

Could he be so selfish as to keep her from himself?

Or could he dare to love her?

Except as the thought entered his mind, it went absolutely blank, darkness settling over his thoughts, his body tensing so much the glass of whiskey shook in his hand, and he had to release the very idea.

He set the glass of whiskey aside. This was getting him nowhere except perhaps at risk for catching a chill. Both of his hands were wrapped around the rim of the tub, his body pitched to pull himself up when his bedchamber door opened. The fact that panic did not immediately set in should have concerned him, but seeing Alice come flying through the door was largely not unexpected.

He sank back into the tub, his hands moving to cover whatever she might have seen.

"I promise he will wish to see me," she was saying—no,

rather yelling—at whoever was chasing her, for someone *was* chasing her.

He could hear the footsteps now that the door was open. They were heavy and plodding, and he pressed a hand to his forehead as his butler came through the door next.

"My lady, he is not receiving visitors. I must insist—"

Ransom held up a hand, stopping Rivers's admonishment. "Quite all right, Rivers," Ransom said, tapping down his grin. "I shall see Lady Alice. Thank you. You may go now."

Rivers, the poor man, appeared scandalized, but really, what was to be done about it? The man's puff of white hair stood straight up over his forehead, his eyes wide, crinkling the loose skin around them. At some point, he must have realized his mouth was open, and he snapped it shut. "Very good, my lord," he said and backed out the door, closing it none too gently behind him.

"Lady Alice," Ransom said now, leaning back in the tub, no longer attempting to hide his body.

If she were here, invading his bedchamber, he might as well let her look. Only she didn't even try. Instead, he took no small amount of delight in watching her fists go to her hips.

"Women will not be given access to the observatory."

Ah. That explained the intrusion.

"How did you know where I lived?" he countered.

Her mouth opened, but she stopped, clearly having been ready to say something else. "That's not relevant. I demand to know why you would not allow women access to the observatory."

He held up a single finger. "First, how you know the location of my home is very relevant. I should like to know if you had scouted it out at some point when you were plotting your nefarious kidnapping scheme or if you have some incredible talent for remembering directions even in the dark." He paused, enjoying the flush that traveled up her neck at his words. "And second, it is not I who is restricting women from the observatory. It is the Astronomers Club."

"The who?"

It was refreshing to watch her face now without the hindrance of the spectacles. He hadn't realized how much her emotions played across her features, and he swore never to allow her to wear them again.

"The Astronomers Club. It's headed by a Lord Dalton, and it's their observatory. They raised the funds that build the thing. They set the rules for admission."

She took a heated step forward but seemed to finally realize he was in a bath and halted, her gaze flying wildly away from him. Interesting. She hadn't been so shy that night in the boat. His body tightened at the memory alone, and he was suddenly glad she wasn't looking at him.

"Then why would you give them money for their observatory if they were to enforce such arcane rules?"

"Because I'm afraid such rules are not arcane no matter how much you might disagree with them."

Her eyes came back to him now, the fury on her face telling him she cared not for modesty. "Excuse me." He'd never heard her voice so low and flat.

"Was it not you yourself who told me of the gatekeepers of science? The men who decide how much and when women are allowed to engage in the study?"

"Yes, but—"

He held up a hand to stop her. "And wouldn't it be a boon to have an ally among them?"

She crossed her arms over her chest now. "If that ally would make an effort in our favor. *Any* effort at all."

It was getting harder not to enjoy her show of strength, her tenacious spirit, and he had to consciously keep his lips from twisting into a grin he was certain she would find antagonizing.

"Ah, I see where you've misunderstood." He held up his hand again, the cold bath water forgotten as she continued to glare. "Providing these gentlemen with the funds to build the observatory is the effort." He picked his hand up now as she opened her mouth to speak, and the gesture was enough to hold her silence, but he knew not for long, so he continued. "I can't earn the trust of these gentlemen if I do not make some kind of overture. My contribution to the observatory is a way for me to build rapport with these gentlemen and enact change in a way I've never been able to do before."

Her lips were still parted from her last attempt to speak, and she stood like that, mouth open, arms crossed, eyes glaring, for several moments until it seemed as though what he had said finally sank in.

Her arms dropped, loose at her sides and finally she blinked. "You would do that?" Her voice was much softer now, almost wondering.

"It's the least I can do." He hoped she could hear the earnestness in his voice. "I watched my aunt Emma trail after my uncle Bart for nearly thirty years. Never once did she get any recognition for assisting him in his studies. The least she can be afforded is access to an observatory."

While her arms had loosened, her face remained lively and now it folded into a look of mild hurt.

He gripped the sides of the tub and leaned forward, concern rippling through him. "What is it now?"

She shook her head softly. "I fear I misjudged you, my lord. I took you for a rogue."

"I am a rogue."

She shook her head again but this time more adamantly. "No, you're not. You actually have a very big heart. You just don't let anyone see it."

At any other time and from anyone else, he would have been able to brush off the statement, but not now and most especially not from her. His resolve—hell, his course in life—had already been shaken by her. Such kindness would be enough to convince him he wasn't being selfish. That he was only taking what he deserved. After all, she thought he had a big heart. For the first time in the whole of his life, he hated what he had done with himself. The reputation he had created. The facade he had constructed to stand between him and love.

Fear gripped him. It was an old fear, but it didn't make it any less biting. It consumed him, flooding his body with an unsettledness that made him want to move as if he could outrun it. So he moved.

He stood, heedless of how near she stood, heedless of her still largely innocent existence. Water sluiced off of him, and he stepped from the tub wrapping a towel around his body, but he didn't hurry about it, giving her time to look her fill if she so wished.

But when he turned back, he found her standing, palms stuck to her eyes, her lips pressed nervously together. And somehow he'd never seen a better sight in his life.

"Is that the position you're going to stay in?" She peeked at him from between her fingers, and he allowed the grin he'd been holding back to come to his lips. "Because it's going to make it very difficult for me to seduce you."

* * *

What was she doing?

This was why she had engaged Ransom in the first place. He was naked. They were in his bedchamber, and—

She dropped her hands completely, but his towel was already firmly in place. Perhaps that was better. Her heart stampeded in her chest, and she thought she might be sick, so maybe it would be wise to take this more slowly.

Unnatural.

The letter writer's words ran through her mind in a sickening loop. Not now. She needed what little confidence she had to get through this. The idea of being seduced was so sterile and rational, but the actual act was nerve-racking.

Would he find her desirable?

She recalled that first night in the carriage and what he had said. That he would need to desire her to seduce her. She swallowed now, her gaze following him around the room.

She'd forgotten all about the observatory and the Guild meeting, her eyes unable to leave him. She hadn't expected him to be so…muscular. His back was to her, and she traced the outline of muscles as he moved, her eyes following the curves and valleys. His arms were just as interesting, the muscles there toned and distinct. She didn't know what it was that gentlemen did all day, but whatever Ransom did had honed his body into a fascinating specimen.

She choked, her own thoughts seeming to constrict her throat.

Suddenly the nervousness vanished, and her eyes narrowed involuntarily.

Ransom was fascinating, and a pulse began low in her stomach, anticipation traveling up her arms.

He stopped at a small cabinet in the corner and pulled the stopper from a bottle of amber liquid.

"Isn't it a little early?"

"Not for the day I'm having," he muttered.

She raised an eyebrow, a gesture rather unlike her but then she hadn't been in an earl's bedchamber before. It wasn't as though she made a habit of intruding into an earl's home contrary to what the butler might think.

She gave herself a moment to look around, taking in the

fine furnishings and soft infusions of color in the dark green drapes at the windows and the swirls of greens and soothing navy in the carpet under her feet. It was masculine yet quiet and comforting, and she wondered how often he retreated to this room. Her eyes traveled to the bed then, and she looked quickly away.

How many other women had been in this room? How many other women had he brought to his bed? Lain there tangled in the sheets, their bodies sweaty and spent?

Somehow she didn't believe any had been there. Like that night in the garden, she somehow sensed she was intruding on hallowed ground.

"What kind of day have you had?" she asked, forcing her thoughts away from the torturous ones she seemed to wish to plague herself with.

He surprised her by turning about with two glasses in hand as he made his way across the carpet to her. "A rather surprising one, I'm afraid." He offered one of the glasses to her.

This moment could not get any more awkward, so she accepted the glass, sniffing tentatively at its contents and trying so very hard not to stare at his chiseled chest and its dusting of dark hair.

Was she salivating? Was this normal?

She took a small sip of her drink to distract her wandering thoughts. It burned but pleasantly so, and she let out a small gasp of surprise. "Oh, that's quite good."

He eyed her over his own glass as he took a sip and after swallowing said, "Have you never enjoyed spirits?"

"I've never enjoyed much, but this is rather pleasant." She peered into her glass. "What is it?"

He didn't answer her right away, and she looked up to find him watching her, a faraway expression on his face. The anticipation that had been crawling along her skin suddenly dived deeper into her, splashing through her like a lightning bolt ricocheting around her body.

"Whiskey," he said, but his voice was as far away as his expression.

What did he see on her face? Why did he study it with such intensity? Suddenly she longed for her spectacles back, but he hadn't returned them that night on the boat, and she hadn't asked for them. Some part of her wanted him to keep them. No one had ever had a piece of her, and she liked the idea that he might be the first.

He plucked the glass from her hand then even though she hadn't finished it. He set both glasses on a table by the abandoned tub with a perfunctory knock against the wood, and she couldn't help but feel he had made some kind of decision with the knocking of glass against wood.

This sensation was further confirmed when he came back to her, pulled her into his arms, and kissed her.

Thoroughly.

She didn't hesitate. She had let her insecurities get the better of her before but not now. She didn't know if it was her smoldering anger at the injustice of the observatory or the letter writer himself that burned somewhere deep inside of her, fueling her anger and passion, but when Ransom kissed her, she threw her arms around his neck and stood on tiptoe to press her body against his.

He tasted of whiskey and smelled of sandalwood soap. His hair was still slightly damp as she ran her fingers up his neck, tracing the corded muscles there. Her heart thundered, and her stomach clenched, her fingers moving with unthinkable slowness, exploring his back and shoulders.

She had never touched him like this.

He had touched her most intimate parts, but she had never so much as touched his cheek, and now to have this expanse of bare skin under her palms had her body teetering.

The muscles she had studied with her eyes were even more interesting when explored with her fingers. She wished she could say she memorized every curve, but his lips were far too distracting for that.

His lips and his hands, apparently.

She wasn't sure how he had managed it or when, but the bodice of her gown suddenly loosened, the sleeves falling from her shoulders as the garment came unbuttoned. She let go of him only long enough to let the sleeves drop down the rest of her arms, and it fell away from her, the heavy skirts swishing along her legs like a whisper.

She was hardly naked and not once did she feel a spike of vulnerability. In fact, she felt only frustration simmering along the edges of her desire that there was still her chemise, corset, and stockings between them. Not to mention the towel still wrapped around his waist.

Instead of putting her arms back around his neck though she skimmed them down his waist and hips, skirting the edge of the towel. She was rewarded with a groan as he deepened the kiss, tilting her back in his arms until she was forced to hang on to him. The way their bodies were pressed together shifted, and she could feel him now, hard against her stomach, and she shivered in response, her body clenching at only the thought of what he might do to her.

That night in the boat she had felt the things she had only read about, and she knew with certainty that the text she had read had only described the mechanics of the act. The actual deed was far more perilous with emotions, and suddenly her heart beat with an eager steadiness.

"Ransom." She moaned his name as his lips left hers.

At first she thought he would trace kisses down her neck, along her collarbone, but he stepped away from her entirely. It was a moment before she could gather herself, her eyes blinking open and yet unseeing.

Finally she brought him into focus and was startled by the tightness of his features, the careful watchfulness about his eyes.

"Alice, I want to make sure you know what you're doing. If we proceed, your reputation will be ruined."

The way he watched her, his eyes so worried, she almost felt as though he cared about her, but no one had ever cared about her. The sensation was overwhelming and confusing, and yet she had never felt more seen in all of her life.

Slowly she reached up, and keeping her eyes locked on his, she slipped the metal clasps that held her corset together free one at a time. His eyes narrowed the smallest of degrees as the first clasp slipped free. At the third one, he swallowed, his eyes never moving from her fingers. The corset fell to the floor, but she didn't stop. Reaching up, she pushed the straps of her chemise from her shoulders, letting the whisper-thin garment join her corset on the floor.

The cold air washed over her body, and instinctively she wanted to wrap her arms around herself, but she wouldn't do it. She wanted him to see her body, and she wanted to watch him as he did. She stood in only her stockings, and for the first time ever, she wished she were wearing something more alluring than her practical walking shoes.

But she kept her gaze on his and watched as finally his eyes lowered, his own gaze sweeping down her body. Every part of her seemed to heat as his gaze traveled down over her breasts and stomach and thighs.

She wished he would speak. She wanted him to tell her he thought she was beautiful, that he thought her desirable, that he...wanted her.

But he didn't speak. Instead he picked her up and carried her to the bed.

Somewhere along the way the towel was lost and to have

his naked body pressed against hers was like touching fire, but she couldn't stop. The dusting of hair along his chest grazed her nipples, and her body tightened, winding almost to a single point of pure pleasure. Her legs parted for him, and he fit between them as though he were meant to be there.

She still wore her stockings and walking shoes, but he didn't seem to care as he continued his sensual assault on her body. Like she had explored the muscles of his back with her fingers, he explored her with his mouth, cruising down along her neck, biting kisses of fire along her collarbone, sucking her aching nipple into his mouth.

But he kept going, lower and lower. He planted kisses along her hip bones, down the curve of her thigh. He slipped from her grasp then, and she was forced to clutch at the bedclothes beneath her, her back arching away from the mattress as he discovered parts of her body that had never been touched the way he touched them, never caressed, never worshiped.

And then his mouth touched her there.

She came up entirely, her hands gripping the back of his head, her body thrumming with desire.

"Ransom." She choked out his name, her throat closing as desire swamped her.

It wasn't enough. She couldn't contain the feelings he invoked in her, and she fell back against the pillows, letting him take her. Her climax was nothing like the one she had felt in the boat. This one was sharper, fuller, and seemed to reach inside of her, wrapping itself around her core, but it wasn't enough. Even as her body flushed with satiation, she knew it was something else.

She was readying herself for him.

As if he knew, as if he understood, he came up and slipped inside of her with one thrust, filling her, stretching her. She expected pain, but it wasn't that. It was as though her body adjusted, accommodating him, welcoming him.

"Ransom."

He pressed his lips to her throat, her jaw, her cheek, her mouth, swallowing her mewls of desire as her body tightened—impossibly—again. His hands swept down her sides, toyed with her aching nipples, cupped her heavy breasts, swept over her hips, pulling her closer to him with every thrust.

"Oh God, Ransom," she cried as climax broke over her again, but this time she felt his release, felt him come undone in her arms, and even though she was nothing but sensations in that moment, she couldn't help but think how natural it felt when he collapsed in her arms.

CHAPTER 11

*H*e woke with a start, his senses cataloging the space around him.

He was in his bedchamber, in his bed, definitely naked, and afternoon sunlight slanted through the window where the drapes didn't quite meet. Judging by the angle though he would have wagered it was late afternoon and perhaps early evening.

And Lady Alice Atwood lay sprawled across his chest.

She was also definitely naked with the exception of her stockings, and—God, had he not even removed her shoes?

He should ease out from under her, take off her shoes, and find her a blanket or something, but instead, he tightened his arms around her and closed his eyes, enjoying the uncomplicated sensation of simply holding her.

What had happened to him? Their lovemaking had been frenzied and heated. For the first time in a very long time, he had felt alive, grounded and present like he hadn't been before. God, what had she done to him?

Now she really was in his home. Fully. In his bed where he'd never taken a woman before. Having a woman in his home had always felt like a violation but not with Alice. He hadn't missed the unmistakable shift inside of him when she had tumbled through his bedchamber door, his unpleasant day falling away at the mere sight of her.

Not for the first time that day did he think about marrying her, and the guilt swarmed him as if it had been lying in wait. He felt the tension ripple through him, dispelling the ease their lovemaking had generated.

Alice stretched as if sensing it, and the hand that had been resting on his chest began to explore, sliding up and—

He caught it in his own but not before she said, "Whatever that thought was, I suggest you banish it for the time being."

Her words were muffled, but it only made him smile more.

"I was just thinking how I've never had a woman in here. I feel rather violated."

She sat up so quickly her hair came loose from its pins, the front part falling around her face in a soft halo. He went completely still. Even though he had made love to her, he hadn't taken the time to take her hair down. This was the closest it had come to falling to her shoulders, and he was arrested by the sight of it.

"You can't mean that."

He put his arms behind his head. "I do very well mean it. I've never been so intruded upon—"

She cut him off with a wave of her hand. "Not that. I meant the other bit. You've never had a woman in your home?"

"Of course I haven't."

Her face turned scarlet, and her eyes were suddenly everywhere except looking at him. He sat up and gently took her arms to bring her back to him. "Hang on now, darling. What's so important about whether or not I've had a woman here?" She tried to pull her arms free, but he held on to her. "Alice, darling, you must tell me what's going on."

She shook her head, more hair falling from its pins. "I didn't realize. I thought, well, with you being a rogue that—" Her words came out quick, almost a staccato and rushed, and she kept looking about as though searching for something. She made to straighten and slip from the bed, and he realized she was looking for her clothes.

He took her chin between two fingers and brought her attention back to his face. "Alice, I have never brought a woman here in all of my roguish years. However, I want to be very clear. Are you listening?"

"I'm listening," she said, but it was mumbled as he still held her chin.

"I always want you here." They were exactly the words he wished to say, and as soon as he spoke them a warmth spread through his chest.

Her eyes were watchful though, and finally she tugged her chin free to say, "I can't tell what part of this is real and what part is because I asked you to seduce me."

It twisted his gut to hear her say that, and instead of responding, he reached down and plucked her walking shoes from her feet, tossing them to the floor. Then he wrapped his arms around her and drew her back down to the bed, holding her close as he pulled a quilt over them.

"Does this make it clearer?" He liked the way she fit against him, and he thought he could very well hold her forever.

"Yes, it rather does." Her hand lay flat against his chest, and he wondered if she could feel his heart beating. There was a second of silence before she said, "Do you really feel violated?"

"Yes, entirely," he said without hesitation. "What on earth did you say to Rivers to get past him?"

"I asked him if his mother knew how he treated ladies." He could hear the smile in her voice, and he couldn't stop his own smile. "Men are always so terrified of what their mothers might think."

He stiffened as if the words had struck him, his body reacting without him realizing, and she came up on one elbow above him, her hair hanging in thick curtains about her face.

"Oh Ransom," she breathed. "I wasn't thinking. I shouldn't have—"

He placed a finger against her lips. "Don't apologize. Not for her." He spoke the words even if he couldn't quite grasp the feeling behind them. His mother had taught him things she couldn't have imagined, but he could admit there was still a little boy inside of him longing for her to come home. Alice was probably right then in appealing to Rivers through his mother. "Just promise me this," he said when her eyes continued to search his face. "No more kidnapping earls or intruding into their homes."

"I can't promise that," she mumbled against his finger as she delivered the haughtiest look he'd ever witnessed.

It made him laugh, the very sight of her like that, so incongruous with her own warm personality.

He shook his head. "You're incredible, Alice Atwood." His voice was nearly breathless as he was suddenly overcome with the wonder that was this woman in his arms.

He stopped laughing when he registered the look on her face. She looked not unlike a child, her eyes going wide and round, her lips ever so slightly parted as if in disbelief.

"I am?" Her voice was almost as breathless as his had been, and he hated the vulnerability he heard in it.

He reached up and captured her face in both of his hands as if by holding her there, he could make her understand the truth. "Alice. I don't know everything that happened to you, and I have no right to ask, but I want you to know this. Whatever it was has made you the strong, brave, courageous person you are today. So no matter what they made you believe remember this. It made you into someone truly incredible." Someone he very much feared he was falling in love with. He couldn't say that part. Not yet. Maybe not ever, but it thundered in his chest like a second heartbeat as he dared to imagine what it would be like. To just love her.

But too much danger and pain lay that way, and before she could say anything he drew her down to him and kissed her.

This time when he made love to her he went more slowly. He savored it and her. He drew each stocking slowly down her leg, kissing each inch of skin as it was exposed. He touched his lips to the soft spot at her elbow, the gentle curve at the back of her knee, the pale skin at her wrist. He kissed her—God, when had kissing ever been this *good*? Never.

This time he entered her from behind so he could hold her against his chest, slip his leg between hers as if they could be any closer to one another. He kept one hand low on her stomach as he thrust into her, hard and slow, drawing out each movement until she begged him to make her climax. Only when he couldn't bear it any longer himself did he relent, pounding into her, driving them both to release.

Darkness had fallen truly by the time they stumbled from the bed. He hated sending her home in a hackney, but he couldn't very well be seen escorting her to her front door. He watched as she slipped those damn walking shoes back on her feet, hating every piece of clothing she rebuttoned, refastened, and retied. Each one marked a space that took her further from him.

He wanted more time, but he knew he couldn't have it. Not like this. He was London's most notorious rogue, and she was the daughter of an earl. There was nothing in front of them except marriage, and he had sworn never to enter into it lightly.

But now…now he was desperate to have her. If only for a little longer and whatever that meant.

As she pulled her cuffs into place, he said, "Come away with me."

The words were out before he could stop them, and she looked up, startled, her fingers still on the pearl buttons of her cuffs.

"Go away with you? Where?" Her lips were ever so slightly parted, and he wondered if he had done that. If he had caused her to relax enough to even make that expression.

"To my country home in Yorkshire. The Falls is beautiful this time of year with everything in bloom. We can go there, and no one will know." The idea blossomed in his mind, and his heart beat faster with excitement. He could picture it. The two of them. Alone in the country. Away from the prying eyes of London and this mess with Lord Ridgeway. He would take her away from all of it, and for a brief time, they could be together.

But why did such an idea make his heart hurt? It was what he wanted, wasn't it? Alice's company without the danger of love and attachment?

He closed the distance between them, and he took her hands into his. "You said you were a very good liar. Could you make an excuse to get away for a few days?"

Her eyes watched him as though he might have suddenly made leave of his senses, but she shook her head eventually.

"Sneaking away will be no challenge at all, but rather why should you want to? I shan't wish to cause you such inconvenience because—"

"You're a damn nuisance, Alice Atwood, but you're no inconvenience." He kissed her, thoroughly, and only when he could feel her relax against him did he ease back.

She didn't open her eyes as she said, "All right."

He kissed her again before she could take it back.

* * *

SHE HADN'T BEEN EXAGGERATING when she told Ransom she was a very good liar. It was only fortunate that Adaline returned to town in time for her lie to be plausible.

It seemed Adaline and Ash were to visit Amelia in Kent and had invited Alice to travel with them. Alice wasn't sure why fate had shined down on her in that exact moment, but she wasn't one to pass by the opportunity. She'd written immediately to Adaline and informed her Uncle Herman had taken ill with a mild chill, and it would be best if Alice remained with him to see to his care.

Meanwhile she had told Uncle Herman the exact opposite. That she did indeed intend to travel with Adaline. And so, the lie was laid. Preparation really was key to a good farce.

Adaline had written back to thank Alice for her attention to their uncle and that she would send back a letter once she had seen their sister.

At this, Alice had felt a modicum of guilt. She hadn't seen Amelia since her hasty departure for her wedding to the Duke of Greyfair some months previous, and if she were a truly loyal sister, she would have abandoned her plans with her lover to visit her sister in her new home.

Lover.

The word startled Alice if only in her thoughts and she dropped the book she'd been about to put into her trunks. She wasn't sure how long they would be at Ransom's country estate, and she didn't very well wish to be without a book. The opening night gala at the observatory was more than two weeks away still, and though she thought Ransom should like to be back in London in time for the event, she couldn't help but wonder if he'd like to linger at his country home a little longer.

Still her clumsiness attracted Kathryn's attention as the maid was helping Alice to pack.

"Are you quite all right, my lady?" Kathryn asked, her arms full of Alice's gowns. "You know, I am quite happy to accompany you if that's what's on your mind."

A maid to accompany her was the furthest thing from Alice's mind just then, but she appreciated Kathryn's concern. In fact, it was rather odd to have someone concerned for her well-being. After a drought of concern in the first part of her life, Alice was finding herself suddenly swamped with it.

She set the book down more carefully into the trunk now and smiled. "I assure you I shall be fine, Kathryn, but I thank you for your concern. My sister's maid will be able to see to anything I should need while we're in Kent."

Kathryn gave her a speculative glance, and Alice wondered if she'd made a faux pas. She knew very little about how maids worked, and she wondered if it would be unheard of for Adaline's maid to assist Alice while they were traveling.

This line of pondering was made even more confusing by the fact that it was entirely imaginary. Alice would not be with her sister at all, but Kathryn didn't know. She bent to her trunk and stuffed a satchel of drawing pencils in next to her books to hide her face and hopefully her rampaging thoughts.

She straightened and brushed at her skirts. "If you'll excuse me, I must go speak with my uncle."

She didn't miss Kathryn's quizzical look as she slipped out into the corridor. Alice really must get better at hiding her thoughts from the servants. She must have lost her talent for it somewhere, and she suspected the blame lay at Ransom's feet.

Moments later she rapped on the door of Uncle Herman's study and waited for her uncle's befuddled cry to enter.

She opened the door to find him hunched over his desk, his nose quite literally pressed into the spine of a book, a magnifying glass held to one eye.

"I don't know why they make these damn charts so terribly small. How do they expect anyone to be able to read them?"

She made her way over to his desk and bent to see the chart he was studying.

"I think that's a seven," she said after some time.

"Really? I was damn sure it was a nine."

She turned her head. "Perhaps it is a nine." She straightened. "I think your conclusion is correct, Uncle. They shouldn't make these charts so small. What are the publishers thinking?"

He set aside his magnifying glass and blinked owlishly at her. "I say you're right. Do these publishers even read their books?" His bushy gray hair was particularly exuberant that morning, and the small remaining tuft of it at the front of his head stuck up over his forehead like a sail. "I'm sure you didn't come in here to discuss the publishing standards of our times. Is something amiss?"

Alice was quick to shake her head. "Not at all, Uncle. I was just letting you know the carriage will be here soon to take me to Adaline's so we can depart for Amelia's." The lie slipped easily from her lips, and she folded her hands in front of her, the epitome of casual grace.

It was only a boon that she'd been able to show Uncle Herman the note Adaline had sent about accompanying her on her trip to see Amelia. It was just that she hadn't shown him her reply to her sister's offer, the one in which she'd lied about Uncle Herman's health and her need to stay at home.

With neither her sister nor her uncle having reason to be concerned for her absence, she could easily slip away for several days if not a week or more. The thought itself sent a thrill through her, heat racing to her extremities, and she turned away, hoping it hadn't crept up her neck and into her cheeks.

She heard Uncle Herman clamber to his feet, rocking back the generous leather chair he had been sitting in to bumble his way around the desk. Her uncle was a large man, and no matter how reserved his efforts, he always appeared to be a bear rambling through a reception.

She turned to him once she thought she had gained her composure.

It wasn't the physical aspects of her escape that had her overwhelmed, but rather it was everything else. The moment when Ransom had held her face in his hands and told her she was something incredible had been the first time in her life when she'd truly believed the kindness of another person. It was startling and uncomfortable, and it opened a door that frightened her.

She wanted this time away with him. Part of her feared she needed it. Needed him to teach her how to be stronger. How to believe the nice things people sometimes said about her. It sounded weak to rely on someone else to tell her she was good enough, but after spending the whole of her life hearing how much she lacked from those that should have loved her, she could admit a certain desperation to for once —*for once*—know that she was enough.

"Do you have everything you might need then?" Uncle Herman asked, plucking at the pocket of his trousers as if something were wedged into it. He withdrew another magnifying glass and eyed is suspiciously, his gaze traveling back to the desk where he'd discarded the one he'd been using when she'd entered. He shrugged and set the second glass down next to the first.

"I'm quite all right, Uncle. I'll have Adaline and Ash. All will be well." She gestured to the book he'd left open. "You must enjoy your solitude while you can. I think it should be nice to have some uninterrupted time with your studies."

Her uncle spiked his fingers through his hair, plumping it up even more. "I fear I spend too much time in solitude with my studies. That's why I'm lucky to have you, dear."

Her uncle's words were spoken with such casualness, and yet they zinged directly to her heart. No one had ever said they were lucky to have her. No one. She blinked now, unable to find the correct response even as her heart leapt in confused joy.

But her uncle only rambled on. "I hope to be through Markham's treatises before you return, and then we can have a jolly debate on his use of crystals in his deductions." He rubbed his hands together as if this were a truly delightful possibility.

She swallowed the lump in her throat and said, "I should like that very much."

Her uncle's smile was huge, and he leaned down to press a kiss to her cheek. "Off with you then," he said. "I'm sure Adaline awaits!" He said this with a great sweep of his hand and had already turned back to his desk, pulling up his trousers as he did so. He stopped though and looked back. "Oh, one thing, dear girl, whatever happened to your experiment? The one where the catalyst was not affecting the desired result?"

Warmth spread through her again, but this time it was something different. There was something beautiful about it, something heavy with happiness and anticipation, and it was unlike anything she had ever felt before.

She couldn't stop the smile from coming to her lips as she said, "I altered some parameters, and the experiment was a success."

Her uncle's responding smile was broader than hers, but she couldn't help but notice a knowing glint to his eyes. "Well done, girl. Well done." It was the quietest her uncle had ever spoken, and it was as though an understanding of some kind passed between them.

She gave him a nod and slipped out of the room, closing the door softly behind her. She stayed there for a moment and pressed her head to the cool wood of the paneled door. Her heart was doing funny things in her chest, and that unfamiliar pool of happiness swirled in her stomach, making her giddy and sick at the same time.

Finally she drew a breath and straightened, making her way to the front of the house.

She reached the foyer to find her trunks had already been brought down. The unmarked carriage Ransom had hired for their journey hadn't arrived yet, and the plan was for her to meet him in the carriage unescorted so he wouldn't be seen. Such cloak and dagger efforts were thrilling, but more no one had ever undertaken such feats for her, and once again she found herself smiling.

She sat down on her trunks to wait.

And wait.

And wait.

But Ransom never came.

CHAPTER 12

*H*e'd sent word to his staff at The Falls to have the house readied. It wasn't like him to visit his country estate during the season, and he hoped he'd given them adequate time. He'd used that time to hire the unmarked carriage and arrange with his in-town staff to cover for his absence. He'd tried to be vague, saying business matters called him to his country estate, but he found he couldn't lie to his aunt Emma. Not when it concerned Alice.

He knew perfectly well that Aunt Emma had come to regard Alice with a maternal protectiveness, and he didn't wish to have it directed at him.

He had never taken such care with discretion in his other affairs. For one, it hadn't mattered. The ladies he had seduced before had all proclaimed their assignations from the rooftops—or rather from every salon and drawing room in London. Being seduced by the Earl of Knighton had taken on an altogether formidable mantel. Once he had derived pleasure from it, a mark of just how successful he had been at distancing himself from his past.

But not anymore.

Now he found it cold, something that served to separate him even further from everyone else.

Once he thought that was what he'd wanted but now it didn't feel like it. He thought of his title of London's most notorious rogue. Once it was a mark of his progress, the very thing he'd longed to become in order to protect himself.

But now when he thought about his future, he wasn't alone in it. He was with Alice. Something like that would have sent him to a bottle not six months ago, but now the thought settled in his brain with the coziness of a napping kitten.

His mind had settled on that same thought so securely that when he opened the door of his London townhouse for the last time, everything in place, the unmarked carriage waiting at the bottom of the stoop, he didn't see the woman coming up that stoop for several seconds. She had her skirts in her hands, her head bent as if climbing that stoop were the most important thing, and she was determined to get it done efficiently.

It wasn't until she reached the top, a mere five feet from where he stood frozen in the open doorway, that she finally looked up.

And his heart stopped.

His lungs stopped.

Anything in his body that could stop stopped.

Only he spoke then, and he knew everything hadn't stopped because he whispered, "Mother."

His mother gathered the Italian lace pelisse about her shoulders, her pointed chin moving up. "Don't stand in the doorway, Ransom. Do you want the neighbors to talk?"

She pushed past him, giving him no time to move. He continued to stare at the stoop where she'd just been standing until he heard her barking orders at Rivers as though she'd never left Knighton House. He turned back, his mind an utter blank except for the need to discover just what was happening.

He hadn't seen his mother in nearly thirty years. What was she doing here? Why was she here *now*? What was going on?

Rivers stood in the foyer, his arms loaded with the outer garments Ransom's mother had discarded. The poor butler's eyes slid to the right in the direction of the corridor that ran to the back of the house. Ransom started in that direction and caught the end of a declaration being cast toward the rear of the house. In seconds, he came upon a startled maid holding a dusting cloth clutched between her hands, her eyes wide and unblinking.

"Which way did she go?" he asked, hoping the poor maid would find Rivers and the man would help to soothe the woman from whatever torment his mother had cast in her wake.

The maid did little more than point, her trembling finger indicating his study.

He strode into the room two seconds later, his fists clenched at his sides.

He found his mother on the opposite side of the room, flinging back the drapes the staff had only secured in place that morning as he prepared for departure.

"I don't know who you have on staff, Ransom, but you will fire them all without reference. This house is in utter disarray." She turned about, dusting her hands as though the drapes were covered in filth.

She looked up then, and now that she had removed her hat and its plumage of feathers, he could see her face clearly.

It hit him, squarely in the chest. She had more color to her features, but it was still the same face he saw every morning when he was only a small boy, peering over him as she drew him from his trundle bed.

All of the confusion, the hurt, the anger, the resentment—it all suddenly fell away. Like water running off the end of a bent leaf, it simply fell away, and he was left standing there, only one feeling coursing through him.

Gratitude.

His mother had come home.

Finally.

"Mother, what are you doing here?" He could hardly make himself speak. Terror spiked through him at the thought that this might all be a dream. That he would wake up and find it wasn't real. That he would once more lose the conduit to the father he had never known.

A line appeared between his mother's brow, and he realized he didn't know her expressions. He should have. He should have understood what that line meant, but all he could piece together was that her face remained remarkably uncreased. She had a square jaw that gave way to her pointed chin and those wide unblinking eyes that he remembered so clearly. Her dark hair had just been touched with gray at the temples and along her forehead, but she still styled it the same, twisted back along her ears into a small knot.

She was still his mother after all this time, and he didn't realize until then how much he had been waiting for her to come home.

He wanted to be angry. He wanted to tell her exactly what she had done to him, but he couldn't. In that moment, he was just a little boy, a little boy that was *grateful* his mother had finally returned to him.

"It's time you were married, Ransom," his mother said, moving to the bell pull in the corner. "The title requires it." She tugged at the bell pull and moved back toward him, taking a seat on one of the sofas that littered the room.

Finding it odd to feel as though he were towering above

her, he took a seat opposite and leaned forward, elbows to knees.

"Of course the title should require that I marry, but that does not require your presence." He hadn't meant the words harshly, but her eyes widened in surprise. He spoke quickly. "I mean you shouldn't be taxed with having to see to the matter, so what is it that has specifically brought you back?"

"Your marriage greatly concerns the title and the family Shepard. As I am still very much a part of the Shepard family, I take great concern in how your marriage will position this family in society."

He sat up. "I shall have you know I expect to make a proposal in the very near future."

His mother lifted a single eyebrow, and again he was struck by the youthfulness of her face. When she had fled in her grief, he had pictured her consumed by dark clothing, her hair growing gray and then white with her anguish, her face falling to crepe with age, but none of this was true. She looked not a day older than when he'd last seen her. It was almost as if the Italian air had kept her young.

"And who is the lady?"

"Lady Alice Atwood. She is the daughter of the late Earl of Biggleswade." The words slipped easily from his lips, and he felt the rightness in the way they seemed to settle the confusion dancing in his chest.

But then his mother sneered and lifted a hand to her forehead. "Then I see I've arrived just in time." She dropped the hand and laid it gently over the opposite one in her lap, the epitome of grace. "You will not marry this Lady Alice."

Anger surged inside of him, anger and disdain. That she should think she could return only to dictate his future to him when she had chosen to not be a part of his past was irrational, and he would not stand for it.

He opened his mouth to object when a maid entered. He

noted it was not the same one as he had come upon in the corridor, and he wondered if word had spread below stairs about his mother's arrival. His mother demanded tea, and the maid left with an off-kilter curtsy made more precarious by her haste to leave the room.

As soon as the door shut behind the escaping servant, he opened his mouth to continue their conversation. His mother would need to accept his choice in wife as he would not be marrying another.

Except then his mother said, "Your father had certain expectations on whom you should marry."

His fingers curled into his knees as his body tensed into stillness.

If she had said anything else, he would already be informing her of his intention to marry Alice. He would now be speaking those very words, assuring her that her guidance was respected if not warranted. But this. Not this.

His father?

His father had expectations for Ransom's marriage?

"What expectations?" he heard himself say instead.

Instead of declaring his intent right there and then to marry Alice. Instead of telling his mother her thoughts on the subject were not necessary. Instead of saying anything else he asked to hear more, to put more words between him and Alice.

His mother raised her chin, one hand going to the back of her head, fussing with the small knot there. "Your father expected you to marry the daughter of a marquess or duke. Nothing less will do for the Earl of Knighton."

"The daughter of a marquess or duke?" He shook his head. "That's ridiculous. I'm only an earl myself—"

"Do not speak as such." His mother's words flew from her lips with such force it had him sitting back. Her lips had thinned to an angry slash, and the color he had noted earlier was gone from her face now. "I will not sit here and listen to you slander the title. Your father would be ashamed to hear you speak so."

For the second time in a matter of minutes, his mind went utterly blank, only one thought filling the blackness.

His father.

While his aunt Emma was his father's sister, there had been an age difference of ten years between them. It was big enough that Ransom's father had been at school already before Aunt Emma had been old enough to remember her childhood, and so Ransom had grown up knowing only stories told in some degree of separation.

Sitting there in his study, he realized his mother had known his father. Actually *known* him. Loved him enough that when he died, she had fled the life she had built with him. He had somehow known all along that his mother was his last tether to his father, and yet his anger and resentment had kept him from fully understanding it until that moment.

It was suddenly clear and oh so easy to understand. There was nothing left for him to do.

"I apologize, Mother. I did not mean any offense to the title. I should like to hear what you have in mind for my marriage if it was to be my father's wish."

His mother didn't smile. In fact, he wasn't sure if he could recall her ever smiling, but her eyes grew lighter at his words, and something untwisted in him even as something else died.

"Very well," his mother said. "I should like to get started as we haven't much time left in the season."

* * *

HE PRETENDED NOT TO CARE.

He pretended he hadn't spent the past fortnight aching

for Alice. He pretended he hadn't spent interminable hours at his clubs, at The Den where he sometimes hid where only Ash might find him, at the boxing club, which served as his last resort when there was nothing but the release of exercise that would calm his nerves.

As he stood in the middle of the College Park Observatory's opening gala, he pretended none of it mattered.

Because his mother knew best. His mother knew what his father had wanted.

He prodded at the void where his father might have been, but it was still the same empty space, the hole his father's death had left. Ransom had thought his mother would have the power to, if not fill it, then to at least make it less noticeable. So far he hadn't noticed a difference, but he knew if he selected the bride his father had wished for him, it would start to feel better. Finally.

He had no connection to the man except through his mother, and he had to trust that connection no matter what. She must have the answers he'd been seeking. It would only take time.

The gala was hosted on the main floor of the observatory, a sweeping and open atrium designed to mimic the canopy of the sky above it, but tonight it felt cramped and hot. He and his mother had been pressed into a corner. His mother had not been out in society since the death of Ransom's father, but it appeared she had not been forgotten.

The tragic widow, so consumed by grief she'd had to flee. It was quite a role to play, and she played it expertly. He watched her, fanning herself with one hand and holding a flute of champagne with the other. He wanted to feel something. The nearly thirty years of rage he had stored up, the anger, the disappointment, the abandonment. But none of that came. He only felt...empty.

"I say, Knighton, this was rather unexpected." Lord

Dalton appeared at Ransom's elbow, the man's thick white hair especially exuberant that evening.

"It is rather a good turnout," Ransom muttered, wishing he had a glass of something to hide behind.

"At this rate, memberships are sure to climb. We may even be able to install the second telescope ahead of schedule." The words blustered through the man's copious mustaches, and Ransom eased a little away from him.

"Yes, we just might." He realized he scanned the room, his eyes hovering over the crowd, searching for a familiar face, oversized spectacles and too tight hair.

Except she didn't have her spectacles any longer. He involuntarily patted the pocket of his dinner jacket, feeling the slight bulge there, tracing the outline of one lens. He knew he should stop carrying them with him, but for some reason, he couldn't let go. It was the last piece of her he still had, and he drew comfort from their weight in his pocket.

If he couldn't have her, he could at least remember how he had fallen in love once.

"Lord Dalton."

Ransom dropped his hand at the sound of Aunt Emma's voice, his melancholy lifting ever so slightly.

"Lord Dalton," she said again as she pushed her way through the last of the crowd. "This is a lovely reception. It was quite good of you to put it on. I was wondering if I might have a word."

Lord Dalton said something then that was little more than a mutter, and Ransom wondered if it was only a twitching of the man's mustaches and then he was gone, slipping through the crowd as though he were running away.

Which Ransom knew he was.

Aunt Emma's frown was severe. "One day I will get that man to speak to me." She turned to Ransom, and the frown melted away, replaced by a smile of mild annoyance. He could tell by how much of her teeth she exposed. "Ransom, you've been avoiding me. I wonder if this has anything to do with why Lady Alice appears as though she hasn't stopped crying in the past two weeks."

His heart dropped into his stomach, and his throat closed around any air he tried to draw in.

But Aunt Emma wasn't finished. "You didn't break her heart like I thought you would, did you?"

He swallowed, trying to figure out what to say, but words no longer made sense to him, floating around in his head in unshaped sentences.

But he didn't need to speak because just then Ransom's mother stepped out from behind his opposite elbow.

"Emma." She spoke her former sister-in-law's name like she was addressing a disappointing scullery maid.

Aunt Emma didn't say anything at first, her eyes growing ever wider, her lips parted just so much. But then she breathed a single word, so full of fire and loathing even Ransom felt its scorch. "You."

Ransom's mother smiled, oblivious to his aunt's loathing. "So good to see you as well, Emma."

"I didn't say that, Gail," Aunt Emma responded. "If I had said anything at all it would be to ask how you found the nerve to come crawling back here."

Ransom's mother's smile vanished. "I see. You're still as heartless now as you were then."

He could see how quickly the situation was going to devolve and made to step between the women, but he never got the chance. Someone else stepped into the space instead, and his life ended.

"I must speak with you," Alice Atwood said, but he didn't hear her. Not straightaway. He couldn't for she was too beautiful, and he longed for her too much, and there she was, standing directly in front of him, and—

He had to break her heart.

He understood that with a suddenness that broke his own heart. She would fight for him. He knew that. She would go toe to toe with his mother, and he couldn't let that happen to her. She didn't deserve it.

He took his time, letting his eyes drift down her body, noting she wore a gown of the deepest blue, a hue to rival the beauty of the night sky, and it was so unlike her usual attire of drab and severe gowns that he got lost in her for a moment.

But then he raised his chin and remembered who he was. London's most notorious rogue. "I'm sorry. I thought our business had concluded, Lady Alice."

His volley could not have been more direct. He watched as she absorbed his words, as she took in the hurt he had meant to inflict. She would never understand if he had tried to simply explain it to her. She was too logical for that. But he knew a way to convince her because he knew where she was the most vulnerable, and he knew how to make it hurt the most. So he did it. He rejected her.

He wanted to feel like a bastard, but he couldn't. Because the moment the words left his lips, he died. Right there in the middle of the gala, of the opening of the observatory he had worked so hard for, with his mother finally returned at his side, his heart stopped beating, and he didn't want it to start again.

He watched her eyes, those beautiful expressive eyes. For only a second there was shock there, but the shock was replaced far too quickly by understanding and then acceptance. To anyone else, she hadn't moved at all. It might have even been argued that she hadn't heard him. But he knew her too well, had studied her face so carefully for so many months now. He knew exactly how she concealed her pain, just as she had concealed it from her family for so long.

175

She did it now. Every muscle of her face unmoving, her limbs rigid, her fisted hands at her hips. It was all just Alice, but unlike everyone else standing there just then, he knew the truth. Alice wore an armor so thick and rigid no one would ever see her pain.

Except him.

Because he felt her pain as if it were his own.

"Ransom." He wasn't surprised it was Aunt Emma who spoke first, her tone swift and efficient in its rebuke.

But he didn't need her admonishment. He had already felt the worst he could possibly feel.

Only he didn't know that was true because then Alice lifted her chin, and with so much courage it sparked a new pain twisting his chest until he thought he would never breathe again, she said, "It's all right, Lady Wetherby. His lordship is correct. Our business is finished."

Once more she was the woman he had encountered that night in the carriage. Barricaded. Protected. Impenetrable. Because she had to be in order to survive.

He had done that to her. He had forced her back into the defenses she had constructed around herself, and he was far more vile than the rogue he had been.

Alice shifted her gaze to his aunt. "Good evening, my lady." She spoke calmly with a slight bow of her head in farewell.

She picked up her skirts and made to move away but she stopped, her gaze suddenly caught on his mother. Ransom stilled, wondering what she might be thinking then. She didn't know his mother. As far as he knew, she couldn't possibly know who the woman was standing beside him.

But then she turned back to him for one fleeting moment, and the look in her eyes had changed.

He expected pity, disappointment, even loathing, but it wasn't any of those things. It was something far worse.

176

It was empathy.

It all but wrenched his heart from his chest, but it was too late.

She disappeared into the crowd, and his mother put her hand on his arm.

"Come, Ransom. Let us forget this unpleasantness. I'd like you to meet Lord Blankenship's daughter."

CHAPTER 13

*S*he had thought she was numb to it.

This pain, this torture, this hollowness that somehow held the power to suffocate her.

She didn't know how long she stayed in bed after that night at the gala. Days? Perhaps a week. It didn't matter.

Nothing mattered.

The letter writer could glory in thinking he had been correct about her for all she cared. It suddenly didn't matter. It didn't matter that some old curmudgeon thought her unnatural. There was nothing unnatural about this heartache. She knew that scientifically.

It was the reason some animals mated for life, and when left partnerless, lost the will to live. Swans. Swans mated for life. They'd had a pair in the pond at Biggleswade House, but the female had died one winter. She hadn't known of what as she'd been too young, and her mother had felt such things were not for young ladies, but Alice had watched the gardener carrying away the poor dead swan wrapped in a canvas.

The male that was left behind stopped swimming,

stopped eating, floating in the pool of dark water alone. It was as though everything inside of him had stopped even as the world continued on around him.

That was how Alice felt now, and she couldn't stop thinking about that poor swan.

Was she doomed to swim in a pond of her own making, alone for the rest of her life?

She had set out on this experiment to prove she was natural, and in the end, she had determined she was *too* natural. She had succumbed to the oldest sickness on record.

Love sickness, the casualty of which was a broken heart.

She touched her face, tracing her temples and cheeks like Ransom had once done. Everything was just as it once was, and yet nothing would be the same.

She had wanted to prove someone wrong, but in the end, she had discovered something about herself that was probably best left unknown.

She could love. She could love deeply. She had love and passion and desire. She had everything.

Except Ransom.

The door to her bedchamber flew open so unexpectedly Alice sat bolt upright in bed, her loose hair tumbling wildly around her head, blinding her to the intruder that stomped in shortly after the door banged against the wall behind it. The scoundrel went directly to the drapes and flung them wide. Rich, yellowy sunshine flooded the room.

Alice winced even as she struggled to get the rest of her hair out of her face. "What is going on?" she demanded, but it hardly came out as anything as she hadn't used her voice much in days.

When she pulled the last of her hair from her face, she expected to see Uncle Herman looming over the side of her bed, but it wasn't Uncle Herman.

It was Kathryn.

The maid set about tidying the room as though she hadn't just barged into her mistress's room, destroying the sanctuary Alice had constructed in the darkened space.

"Kathryn." Alice tried to admonish the girl, but once again, her voice failed her. She cleared her throat and tried again. "Kathryn, what is the meaning of this?"

The maid pretended not to hear, and Alice realized the woman was singing a tune softly under her breath, something about clouds and rainbows and hearts that have been broken.

"Kathryn." Alice gave more force to her voice, and finally, the maid turned, her arms full of discarded stockings and plates holding the remains of Alice's meager meals, mostly cold chicken and apple cores.

"My lady?" Kathryn asked, blinking as though the picture of innocence.

For a moment Alice felt guilty, as though *she* were interrupting Kathryn.

"I beg your pardon," Alice murmured and then shook her head. "No, that's not it. Kathryn, what are you doing here?"

Kathryn piled the plates in her hand together into a somewhat neat stack. "I'm tidying the room, my lady." She had the audacity to blink now, her eyes wide like some sort of illustration in a children's book.

"But I'm in it." That wasn't what she had meant to say, but she couldn't very well tell a servant she was attempting to recover from a broken heart.

"I see that, my lady," Kathryn said and moved to pick up the gown Alice had discarded when she'd returned home from the gala.

It had been a new gown, a ridiculous splurge she had made after the ladies of the Guild had all decided to attend together. She had wanted to look special that night as if her gown could make her *feel* special. How foolish she had been.

Perhaps the gown could be remade to be a more suitable day gown.

Or maybe she'd drag it out to the garden and light it on fire. That seemed somehow more fitting.

Alice scrambled from the bed, her nightdress catching along her ankles as she attempted to do so. She tumbled more than stepped from the bed, and she forced her long hair from her face once more. This was why she wore it so tightly knotted. It was far too cumbersome and only served to get in her way.

She used the back of a chair to steady herself and shake the last of the tendrils from her face.

"Kathryn, I have no need—"

"Did you know I fancied myself in love once?" Kathryn's head had disappeared into the armoire that housed Alice's gowns, and her voice was muffled, but Alice heard the words as if they were fired from a cannon. She didn't know how to respond so she waited until the maid's head popped free, her brilliant smile firmly in place. "He was the son of a blacksmith, you see. Right fine bloke if I say so." She shook her head. "I almost fell for it. It's a wonderful feeling being in love. It almost makes you miss everything else that's going on around you."

"I beg your pardon." Alice knew the maid was attempting to make a point in a roundabout way, but Alice was not one for the dictates between servant and master. She wanted the woman to speak her mind.

Kathryn scraped the crumbs from the desk Alice had used as a dining table, sweeping the bits into an empty teacup. "My father's a baker, remember?" She gave Alice a sidelong glance. "I thought the son of a blacksmith would have been safe. He's a trade to inherit and wouldn't be coming after me in the hopes of getting my pa's bakery."

Alice shook her head. "I'm not following."

Kathryn set down the teacups she had gathered and wiped her hands on her apron. "I was wrong, and I almost found out too late." Kathryn shook her head. "I almost mistook my man's love for me and not for the steady stream of income he thought he would inherit if he married me."

"How do you know he was only marrying you for your father's bakery?" Alice realized she had gripped the back of the chair now, waiting with rapt attention for the rest of Kathryn's story.

"The idiot had the nerve to tell me I couldn't accomplish anything without him." She gave a bark of laughter. "He thought he had muddled my brain enough with his vows of love and armfuls of flowers." She laughed again, the sound softer now, her head shaking in an almost whimsical manner. She abruptly shrugged and straightened. "I guess I got the better of it in the end."

Alice stepped eagerly around the chair, unable to stop herself. "How is it that you got the better of it?"

Kathryn had moved to sweep the discarded pieces of balled paper Alice had begun tossing at her rubbish bin in the wee hours of some morning when the beating of her heart had grown terribly frightening. It was an awful waste of paper, and she felt guilty now that Kathryn had to pick it up, but alone with nothing but her stampeding heart, it seemed like the perfect distraction.

"Well, I'm proving him wrong, aren't I?" She gestured about her. "I asked my aunt—I mean, Mrs. Marble, to train me as a maid. With training and a good job, I don't need a husband, and my bloke won't have a chance at my pa's bakery." She smiled again, her infectious smile. "And he thought I couldn't amount to anything." The maid shook her hand in Alice's direction, a balled piece of paper crinkling between two fingers. "Know this, my lady. Gents are always thinking they're stronger than us, but if they were, God would have made them have the babies. That's just science, my lady."

Somewhere deep inside of her a bell chimed as Kathryn's words connected with a memory, a memory so soft and precious her mind had tucked it away. Ransom, cradling her face, whispering to her. Telling her her past had made her strong, not broken.

She winced as the memory formed, shutting her eyes against it. She didn't know any longer what was real and what wasn't. Ransom had tried to convince her of his sincerity, but how could she believe him now?

That night at the gala when she had seen the hardness of his face, the way his expression closed as soon as she stood in front of him, it was like she had encountered the rogue she had expected all along.

So then how could she remember their time together as anything more than an act? An act he had perfected over years of playing the charming rake?

The memory fell like a stone through her, falling and falling until it finally crashed into a pool so deep within her she hardly heard the water ripple.

Then she opened her eyes and saw Kathryn standing in front of her, the crumpled paper still in one hand.

"Kathryn, I'm going out." Alice picked her way between discarded shoes and spilled piles of books.

She was nearly to the door when Kathryn called out. "My lady?" Alice turned, her hand on the doorknob. "May I suggest a change of clothes?" The maid swept her gaze down Alice's body.

Alice looked down, remembering her nightdress. She paused in her perusal though. While she recalled the nightdress, she didn't remember the glob of jam on one side and the tea stain on the other. Just how long had she been sequestered in her rooms?

She looked up. "I think you're quite right, Kathryn. And perhaps a bath as well."

* * *

SHE STOOD in front of the dormant fireplace of Lady Wetherby's drawing room and observed the startled, owlish blinking of the assembled women before her.

Their faces had morphed from rapt eagerness when she'd taken the floor to startled concern. Alice knew that expression. She knew it because she'd seen it on her own face once, long ago, when her mother's barbs and her father's dismissals still held the power to affect her.

She hated seeing it on the faces of these women. Over the past several weeks she had come to understand just how remarkable these women were, how strong and intelligent, brave and resilient. To see them cowed by Alice's suggestion only served to prove Ransom was correct, and that only rankled Alice's nerves.

Alice was stronger. She didn't know how she hadn't seen it, but then she supposed she had had nothing against which to compare her own actions. She had thought herself quiet and reserved, guarded and alone. But in fact, it seemed she had been preparing herself for this moment, building a strength that only opposition could forge.

And now she was prepared to take on that opposition if no one else would. She had once feared her studies were at an end, blocked by the men who guarded the one thing that had brought her comfort. But her career in science wasn't at an end at all. She just hadn't seen the path she was supposed to take. At least not then. Ransom had changed that for her.

Lady Wetherby was the first to speak. "You plan to chain yourself to the front doors of the observatory?"

Although this was precisely what Alice had stated, Lady Wetherby's question only served to prove that Alice's endeavor was rather outlandish. For these women. Not for Alice. As soon as the idea had entered her mind, she could picture it perfectly. She even knew where to obtain the chain and lock. But it was obvious her scheme was a step too far outside the bounds for even these women who defied social norms.

"Yes, I do," Alice replied. "If the men who run the observatory shall not give us entrance, then we shall deny them entry in return." She scanned the upturned faces, watching her with such quiet and worried gazes. "I plan to remain chained to the edifice until women are given full access to the premises in equality with their male counterparts."

This brought a small sigh of what sounded like admiration from Melanie Greenawalt, and Alice turned a curious glance in the woman's direction to find her no longer gripped by concern but melting somewhere into quiet wonder. Alice shifted uncomfortably. She didn't wish to be admired for her strength. She wished to infuse these women with just an ounce of it.

They would be so much stronger as a united front, but it seemed she would be striking out alone in this endeavor. Perhaps when she was successful it would inspire these women to more, more courage, more bravery, more daring. It would be a start.

"Do you think this will work?" Lady Wetherby asked, her tone rich with curious hope and not scorned judgment.

Alice raised her chin. "If it doesn't, we'll keep trying. We won't give up the fight until women have equal access to science."

This was met with a flutter of startled gasps, frantic fan waving, and even some hurried, fortifying sips of tea.

"But we've never challenged the men of science before."

This came from Mrs. Muskgrove, a petite woman with dark hair and small teeth who studied botany.

"Exactly," Alice replied, stepping forward to circulate amongst the gathered women. "We've never challenged them. While we may have shown our studies to be just as exemplary as theirs, we haven't revealed to them our strength."

"What strength?" May Greenawalt asked. "Personally, I'm terrified of silly things. Like when people bend the corner of a page to mark their place in a book." She shivered grandly, sloshing the tea she held in her cup. "Nothing is so terrifying as a dog-eared book."

Her sister nodded emphatically beside her.

Alice shook her head. "That is precisely what I mean. Together we are stronger than we are apart. We can fill the gaps the others might be feeling. We can bring a cohesion to the fight that alone we cannot attempt."

"Cohesion?" This from Mrs. Muskgrove again. "Do you mean like how bees work together to create a honeycomb?"

Murmuring followed this question, and Alice spoke above it. "Yes, something like that." She gestured widely. "All of nature is filled with examples of the strength of many versus the strength of one. We have only to emulate it."

This was met with hushed silence marked with periodic bursts of whispered comments.

Alice felt as though she were teetering on an edge, the women's indecision vacillating back and forth, and she could only hope it would fall in the favorable direction.

But then Lady MacDonald, a tall, slender woman with hair so blonde it was almost white, raised a timid hand. "But my husband shall never let me participate in such scandalous behavior."

There was the statement Alice had feared, and she closed her eyes against it and the resulting cascade of consent that rippled through the room. More women joined in Lady MacDonald's statement, asserting their own reluctance to join a protest in fear it would be met with displeasure from their husbands.

Alice felt the edge she had been riding crumple and fall into despair. Her shoulders slumped but only for a moment. She opened her eyes and said, "I completely understand. I shall engage in this endeavor alone so as to protect your reputations."

She turned about the room as she spoke, trying to meet the eye of every woman gathered so everyone would understand her sincerity, her drive and determination to see this thing through. But most avoided her gaze, and she felt the last of her hope crumble away.

"If you will excuse me," she finally said and shuffled through the maze of gathered women in the direction of the foyer.

She felt the sting of rejection, but it was different this time. It was heavy with a collective sadness that overwhelmed her own personal feelings of never quite fitting in. She had no husband to stop her, and she had never been one to aspire to the submissiveness of a lady. But this was something greater. This was a moment of despair for the future of women in science, and she must not carry it personally.

"Alice."

She had almost reached the front door of the Wetherby home when Lady Wetherby called out. She turned, forcing a pleasant smile to her lips. "I'm sorry if I upset anyone, Lady Wetherby. If you should wish for me to no longer attend these meetings, I understand."

Lady Wetherby's eyes widened in momentary confusion. "It's not that at all, Alice. And really, you must call me Emma." She shook her head and continued before Alice could respond. "As I said, it isn't that at all. In fact, this is the liveliest this group has been in ages. I should ask you to speak at every meeting. You'll keep us young." She gave the closed-lip smile of satisfaction Alice was coming to understand she used a great deal when speaking with other members of the Guild.

Alice felt a wash of camaraderie then. Like a warm bath, it enveloped her and almost made her feel at ease. She swallowed. "Then what is it?"

Lady Wetherby's smile bent into a troubled frown. "It's about my nephew. Ransom." She said his name as though Alice might have forgotten it.

But Alice would never forget it. She had tried. That experiment had failed before it had begun.

"What about Lord Knighton?" She refused to use the name even if she couldn't forget it.

Lady Wetherby raised both of her hands and formed a sphere with her fingers as if holding the conversation between her palms. "Well, you see his mother has unexpectedly returned from Italy, and I'm afraid her presence has unintentionally derailed Ransom's plans for his future."

Lady Wetherby had confirmed a suspicion Alice had held since that night at the gala when she'd seen the older woman standing at Ransom's shoulder. So that *was* his mother, returned from Catanzaro. The last hope Alice held that Ransom would come to his senses, that what had happened between them had been real, that something would pry loose this wall that had so inexplicably sprung up between them vanished.

The one connection left to his dead father had returned to his life.

"I suppose his mother wishes for Ransom to wed for the sake of the title." Although she may not have moved much in society, Alice was still aware of the demands of a title. Her own sister, Amelia, had fallen victim to such demands herself, marrying a duke who needed a wife to carry on the lineage.

Only she didn't expect the sharp pain she felt at the words. She was the daughter of an earl, a perfectly acceptable choice for the bride of an earl. Only Ransom hadn't chosen her. He'd rejected her.

But then hadn't she told him she would never marry?

"Yes, it seems she does." Lady Wetherby shook her head again. "I'm sorry to say Ransom's mother has some sort of power over him. Perhaps because of what happened when he was younger…" Her voice trailed off in a mutter of indecision.

It was Alice's turn to shake her head. "It isn't his mother who holds the power over him. It's the fact that she is his last connection to his father."

Lady Wetherby's face cleared, her lips forming a silent *oh* as she seemed to absorb Alice's words. "Ransom's father?" Her tone marked her confusion although its volume suggested a surprise Alice wondered at.

"Yes, his father. Ransom has always wondered about the man and what he would wish for his son. I'm afraid it's a troublesome problem for the earl, one that will likely never be solved, but it's still one he will not give up on." She shrugged. "And if his mother has returned, he's just gotten back the one person who can provide him with any answers." Alice plucked her wrap from the stand by the door. "Good day, Lady Wetherby."

Alice left even though Lady Wetherby's expression as she did so continued to haunt her several blocks away. It was almost as if the woman had discovered a new element.

CHAPTER 14

"*R*ansom, we must talk."

He nearly fell out of his chair. He'd had his feet propped on the low table in front of him, his head thrown back, eyes closed, glass of whiskey trundled precariously between two fingers so that when he heard his aunt Emma's voice, the entire thing had nearly upended.

Not because he hadn't been expecting her. Although he hadn't.

It was the fact that at that moment he was nestled deep within the strictly male, debauched scions of The Den.

"Aunt Emma, what on earth—"

She raised a hand. "Save me the theatrics. A men-only edict is not going to stop me when it is a matter of most importance." Aunt Emma looked about her, her nose slightly wrinkled in disgust as she slowly sank to the chair adjacent to his own. "Besides, it's not as though seeing the inside of the place has made me wish to rally for women's member-ship. Where are we sitting exactly? Is this supposed to be some kind of study?"

Ransom had been hiding in the exclusive upstairs lounge

of The Den in the corner deemed the library for its potted ferns and dusty shelves of books. "Something like that," he muttered.

She placed her reticule in her lap with an emphatic plop, placing both hands on top of it as though she didn't wish to know more. "Now then I should like to discuss Lady Alice."

He was afraid of this. He set his glass aside carefully. "Aunt Emma, I know—"

"No, you don't actually. Alice has told me as much, and I'm here to correct the issue."

His gaze flew to hers. "Alice has told you what?"

"About your father. Ransom, you've never said anything to me about it. About how you wish you'd known his intentions for you."

He hated how her eyes crinkled in concern, how that line appeared between her brows, so deep and troubled.

"I didn't wish for you to fret. I know there was a great age difference between the two of you, and I didn't wish for you to feel as though you failed."

"But that's just it. I haven't failed you." With this pronouncement, she plucked apart the strings of her reticle and withdraw a parcel wrapped carefully in twine. She held it out to him. "If you had only asked, I would have given you these straightaway."

Upon closer inspection, it wasn't a parcel. It was a bundle of letters. He took them automatically, the aged paper crinkling softly in his grasp. "What are these?"

"They're from your father. I had just wed when you were born, and I must say it transformed your father. He quite suddenly struck up a correspondence with me as though my wedding marked me as an adult or some such thing. But perhaps it was because he was quite overcome by your arrival and wished to tell someone about it." She prodded his knee. "Go on. Look."

He stared at the bundle in his hands, suddenly unable to pull the bow loose from the twine, let the string fall away. These letters were from his father. His father had touched them, written them. They contained his father's very thoughts and feelings. It was a direct route to the man he had lost. These weren't memories filtered through others' consciences. These were real and terrifying.

He swallowed. "How will these help?"

Aunt Emma could not know of what he spoke. Of this pain he had carried since his mother's return. Of this agony that tore at him. He wanted more than anything to do as his father wished, to carry a part of the man forward, but his heart ached. It longed for something just out of his reach.

Alice haunted his dreams. Literally. He couldn't close his eyes without seeing her, and it meant he was not only slightly drunk most days but also bone tired. It was all he could do to keep her from his thoughts and yet…

He looked up to find Aunt Emma studying him. "You love her, don't you?" She shook her head before he could respond, a small, knowing smile coming to her lips. "I never thought you would fall in love, Ransom. I should have known it would take someone like Alice to bring you to it." She tapped the letters again. "Read them."

He tore open the bundle now, curiosity driving a fire in him that he hadn't felt in days. He dropped the twine to the low table in front of him and opened the first letter, his eyes scanning quickly.

His father's penmanship was neat and unhurried, speaking of a patience Ransom realized the man had passed down to him. It was odd seeing his father's handwriting like this. Ransom had seen it any number of times since taking over the title's ledgers and accounts, but this was different. This wasn't just a retelling of estate business. This was personal.

His father wrote of Ransom's impending birth with a fevered excitement that was clear in his words. It made Ransom read faster, pouring over the first three letters quickly, setting them aside before stopping at the fourth letter. The letter that marked the occasion of his birth.

8 May 1842

My darling sister,

I write to you today with news that has eclipsed my very heart.

My son has finally arrived.

Ransom Elias Daniel Montgomery Shepard arrived this morning in the early hours of dawn with a screeching cry that I assure you foretells of his great strength.

Emma, I know I should be thinking of the security of his future, but when I first saw his face, I only wished for one thing for him in this life.

Love.

That is it, dear Emma. I wish for Ransom the kind of love I have found with his mother and the kind you have found with Bart. For that is the greatest thing, isn't it? To find someone with whom you can travel this path of life. It is my greatest wish that my son finds her one day. His equal, his match, his companion, and his champion. I wish for him a partner to be his every desire, his every hope, his every thought, his everything.

I will write more. I promise. But for now, I desire simply to hold my son.

I do hope you and Bart will come visit as soon as possible. I know you will love him too.

Your fondest brother,

Everett

Ransom looked up from the letter, aware that tears had filled his eyes but unable to stop them. "My father wrote this?"

He noted how damp Aunt Emma's eyes had grown as

well. "Yes, he did. I'm only sorry I didn't share it with you sooner, Ransom."

He returned his gaze to his father's words, the present warring with the past. "Did my father ever say anything about marrying the daughter of a duke or marquess?"

The words sounded odd to his ears, and he realized how strange a request that would have been. Had he been so swept up in the possibilities his mother's return represented that he hadn't thought this through?

He looked to his aunt once more to find the line had returned between her brows.

"Of course not. Your father was never so prejudicial when it came to titles. He only wished for you to find love. Did your mother tell you something different?"

He could only nod, the realization of his own weakness stopping the words in his throat.

"You know your mother fabricates truths, Ransom," Aunt Emma went on. "She tells herself lies that give her comfort. It's a sad state, but that's how she's always been. I think she may have been jealous of your father's propensity to love so easily." She sat forward then and gripped the arm that held his father's letter in both of her hands. "And you have found love, haven't you, Ransom?" He saw the hope in her eyes, the earnestness of her question.

"I have." He whispered the words, afraid if he spoke them too loudly it would all disappear.

But it had disappeared, and it was his fault. He had spent his whole life running away from love, and now that he'd found it, he'd pushed it beyond his reach.

He gathered his father's letters, his hands shaking. "I must go. I need to get to Alice."

He was surprised when Aunt Emma leaned forward and helped him furiously gather his father's letters, wrapping the twine about them once more. He would read them again, more thoroughly and at his leisure, but for now he must get to Alice.

"Yes, you'd better, and I recommend you hurry. You'll want to tell her how you feel before she's arrested."

This stopped him cold. He seized Aunt Emma's arm. "What are you talking about?"

His aunt sat up, her expression blank. "Alice intends to chain herself to the entrance of the observatory to protest the lack of accessibility for women scientists."

"She's going to what?" The idea of Alice chaining herself to a building made him smile, and he had to exert a great deal of effort not to display his amusement at the thought.

Aunt Emma nodded, clearly attempting to hide her own smile. "Indeed, she plans to protest the membership terms of the observatory. She will be quite unavailable when she's arrested for the act, so you may wish to speak with her immediately."

Ransom surged to his feet and was two steps away when he stopped and turned back to his aunt. "Why did you come find me here of all places?"

It was odd seeing his aunt standing there in the corner of The Den where he preferred to retreat. Seeing his aunt standing there in the private drawing room that was modeled after a library he realized how blatantly false the facade was. It was nearly laughable. Aunt Emma didn't seem the least uncomfortable in the charade just then.

"I wished to speak with you without the influence of your mother." She frowned. "It's rather strange having the woman back in your life. I should have preferred it if she had stayed away." She shook her head. "I know she's your mother, Ransom, but she's been considerably awful to you, hasn't she?"

Ransom retraced his steps and took his aunt's hands into his. "She may have given birth to me, but the only mother

I've ever had is you, Aunt Emma." He kissed her cheek softly and left before she could see the tears that had returned to his eyes.

* * *

SHE WAS NOT SO CONSUMED by her determination to see equal access to the observatory for women as to not attempt a less drastic approach first. It was only luck that she had seen Lord Dalton that night of the gala when he gave the opening remarks. Now she had a face to put with the name, and she knew who her target was.

She did, however, attempt to find him where Lord Dalton could not refuse her audience unless he should choose to give the cut direct to an earl's daughter in the middle of a ball.

Looking around her, she rubbed at her arms, hoping to quell the unease that prickled along her skin. Although she was determined to see this through, she had no desire to be trapped in the middle of a ball. The last ball she had attended had been the one where Ransom had given her dancing lessons and kissed her in the shadows under the stars.

She swallowed, hating the immediate sting of tears at her eyes. Squaring her shoulders, she tried to remember what Kathryn had said. Sometimes it was a woman's prerogative to prove the naysayers wrong. No matter who they were.

She picked her way through the crush on this side of the ballroom. The season was winding down, but that hadn't prevented a smashing success for the hostess, Lady Brody. It was only luck that Alice had found the invitation unanswered on the hall table when she'd returned to Biggleswade House the afternoon of the Guild meeting.

She only wished Adaline was in town so Alice could have asked her if it was likely Lord Dalton would be there. Adaline hadn't sent word she'd returned though, and Uncle Herman had been noticeably absent for days. She felt a pang of guilt at thinking her uncle may have wrongly assumed she was gone from the house as well as she hadn't spoken to him again after Ransom hadn't appeared that day to take her away. Her poor uncle was probably going about his research under the assumption that he was alone in residency at the house. Poor man. She could admit she would have felt better knowing he was there that night as he would have accompanied her if she'd only asked.

It needn't matter. She could do this on her own.

She'd made it to the other side of the ballroom by then and could peek inside the adjacent card rooms. It was difficult to pick out Lord Dalton even though his copious white mustaches and fluffy mane of stark hair should have been easy to find, but the room was cloudy with cigar smoke.

She coughed immediately upon entering the room, drawing every eye in the vicinity in her direction. For a moment, she froze, so unused to being quite so seen that she felt momentarily captured by their gazes. But then someone laughed, and a glass clinked glass in a roar of cheers, and the moment dissolved around her.

Pressing her hand to her nose and mouth as if to help filter the smoke, she scanned the room again, finding Lord Dalton off to the side, speaking amiably with a young man with bushy muttonchops.

She made her way directly to him, stopping only when his attention drifted to her. "Lord Dalton, I must have a word with you."

He eyed her like a scullery maid who had the audacity to knock at the front door. "I'm sorry, girl, but I have no interest—"

"I'm not a girl. I'm Lady Alice Atwood. You may address me by my title." The uneasiness that had stolen over her upon entering the ball seemed to have vanished, the immediate rejection in the older man's eyes sparking a defense in her she had thought not possible.

"Lady Alice Atwood, was it?"

There was something strange about his eyes. When she had spoken her name, they had widened just the slightest bit as though in recognition, but that couldn't be possible. She had never been introduced to Lord Dalton, so there was no way for him to know who she was.

"Yes, and I should like to speak to you about an oversight in regard to the Observatory at College Park."

"Oversight?" Lord Dalton turned more fully to see her now, his eyebrow rising in mock concern as he clearly tried to stop a smirk.

"I hope it's an oversight and not a blatant disregard for the intellectual prowess of the female sex." Her voice had risen at some point, and she knew she was drawing the attention of the card players around her.

She no longer heard the low murmur of conversation and soft buzz of idle chatter, the clink of glass, the puff of smoked cigars.

Lord Dalton watched her now with barely veiled hostility. "Lady Alice, I regret—"

"Excuse me, Lord Dalton, but I believe I have already secured the lady's next dance. You will forgive me for intruding."

That voice. That voice that pierced her heart, that shattered the calm resolve that had stolen over her, that—

Made her so instantly, infuriatingly angry.

She spun about. "I have not promised you a dance."

She didn't bother with a greeting, but her anger died instantly at the sight of him.

Ransom.

Dressed in his finest evening attire, stark black and crisp

white that only served to accentuate the blues of eyes, those terrible blue eyes that hypnotized her, that had tricked her, that had made her fall in love.

Worse, he was smiling. That warm, playful smile she loved so much.

What was he doing here? Why was he doing this? She'd promised him no dance. He knew perfectly well she couldn't dance at all. Their one lesson had hardly been met with success. She should have known it wouldn't because she had the horrible tendency to become perfectly helpless the moment he touched her.

Just as he did now when he drew her arm through his.

"Would you please excuse us?" He said this to Lord Dalton, but he obviously didn't expect a response as he was already leading her away.

And she let him. Damn and blast, what was wrong with her?

He had already steered her out into the corridor beyond when she thought to pull her arm free.

"Ransom," she hissed. "What are you doing? I—"

"Ransom, what is the meaning of this?"

Alice stopped at the icy cool voice that cut over her exclamation. She wasn't surprised to see Ransom's mother standing not two feet from them, a champagne flute in one hand. She crooked a single eyebrow much like Ransom did sometimes, and Alice wondered if he'd inherited the expression from her. Only on Ransom it was playful. On his mother it was sinister.

"Mother, I—"

"Ransom, I shall not stand for your impudence. I—"

"Oh shut up." Alice hadn't meant to yell it, but she really was quite sick of this woman. "It's my turn to voice my grievances to Ransom." She didn't know what came over her, but she was suddenly seized with an anger so great she reached out and shoved the woman out of their path, spilling champagne down the woman's silk gown. She let out a cry of surprise that drew even more attention in Alice's direction, but she didn't care. "Wait your turn," she growled, and this time it was she who pulled Ransom away.

They had made it not more than two steps when a gentleman separated himself from the crowd. She stopped, confused. The man was hardly taller than her, and his paunch pushed at the buttons of his peach waistcoat. His hair was flat and sparse, his face pockmarked and puffy.

"Excuse me, Knighton. The name's Ridgeway and—"

Alice pointed at Ransom's mother. "You can wait your turn behind her."

The man's mouth fell open uselessly, but she didn't wait for a rebuttal. In fact, this time she didn't stop until they were through the terrace doors and out into the quiet of the garden beyond.

If he had something to say, he would say it here, under the stars. That was where they seemed to speak to each other best, and if this were to happen, she would wish it to happen here. If he were to explain his reasons for rejecting her, she would want to have the stars to comfort her.

But instead he said, "I love you, Alice, and I've come to beg your forgiveness."

Her lips parted. She wasn't able to stop them as the shock spread through her body, and then she said, "You idiot."

The words shot from her mouth, startling her into silence. She had thought herself angry. Angry with him. Angry with the mother who had dismissed her. Angry with the father who had rejected her. But as those two words sprang from her lips, she realized that while she had begun this journey to be seduced, something else had happened instead.

She had learned to trust again.

London's most notorious rogue had taught her how to trust. And in that moment, when he said he loved her, she believed him, swiftly and entirely.

He took a step closer to her, his hands pressed together as if he were begging. "Yes, I have been an idiot, and I can only hope that you'll forgive me. You see my mother—"

"Your mother returned from Italy, I know. Your aunt told me as much."

His eyes roamed over her face as if he were desperate to take in all of her expression at once, any hint of what she might be feeling, and once, she might have closed herself off but not anymore. Now she let him look. "Yes, but did she tell you of my mother's demands?"

Her eyes widened. "Demands?"

He nodded, and she realized he was much closer now as she had to look up to see him. She smelled his sandalwood soap, and she thought she would suffocate for the desire that welled up in her in response. "She told me it was my father's wish that I marry the daughter of a marquess or a duke, and I believed her."

She shook her head. "Are you saying that wasn't true?"

Instead of answering her, he withdrew a small, folded piece of paper from his pocket and extended it to her. She peered at it, uncertain.

"Read it," he said, and she realized it was a letter.

Tentatively she took it between two fingers before carefully unfolding it, touching only the very edges of it as if whatever it contained might hurt her more. She read it, once, twice, thrice, but the words swam together, and she realized she was crying.

"Ransom," she tried, but the tears had clogged her voice.

"My father, Alice. It's from my father."

She nodded, but the tears were coming too quickly now for any more words.

"My father wanted me to find love, Alice. Not a duke's daughter. Just love. My mother lied to me, and I was so desperate to believe I had a piece of my father that I believed her. You were hurt because of it, and I will always regret that. I can only hope you can for—"

She reached up and pulled his head down, her lips crushing his in a kiss as she tried to stop his words. His arms came around her, lifting her against him until she could feel all of him, but most of all his heart pounding like hers did.

"Ransom," she finally managed some moments later. "Do not ever apologize for that woman. Promise me. For the rest of our lives, do not ever make an excuse for her." She watched his face, lit only by the moon and the stars, and she thought of that night so long ago now when they stood in a different garden.

Could she have known then that this moment would come? That they would be standing here tonight? She hadn't thought it possible, but then a lot of things had happened to her that hadn't seemed possible. And it was likely all because someone had taught her to believe in herself.

His eyes roamed over her face again as if he couldn't believe what was happening either. "The rest of our lives? Do you mean that, Alice?"

"I do. That is if that's why you wished to speak to me. I must admit I haven't practice with this sort of thing, but I believe when two people love each other the next practical step is marriage, so if—"

"Do you, Alice?" That playful grin she loved so much was on his face, moonlight sparking off his white teeth. "Do you love me?"

"Of course I do, you idiot. Don't you love me?"

His laugh rumbled beneath the palms of her hands where she had pressed them to his chest. "Of course I love you, Alice Atwood." His face sobered, and his eyes grew pensive.

"I only worry about the other thing Aunt Emma told me. You have plans to chain yourself to the observatory in protest?"

Her euphoria was quashed almost instantly as she remembered the worried looks of the other members of the Guild and how they feared their husbands' reactions to such scandalous behavior. She made to step away from Ransom, but he held fast to her arms, keeping her pressed against his chest.

"I'll not change my mind, Ransom. Women have as much of a right to use that observatory as men, and I will not stop until they do."

She thought he would be angry, but his face didn't show anger. It showed pride. In her.

She thought when someone finally loved her she would feel whole, unbroken, but she'd been wrong. The look Ransom gave her then was not one of only love. It was one of pride, one of happiness, one of expectation, one of knowing, and it was so much more than she had ever dreamed.

But he wasn't done because then he said, "I would never dream of stopping you, Alice. I would only ask that you do something first."

CHAPTER 15

he chain was far heavier than she had expected, and she hadn't counted on the rain. Even under the shelter of the observatory's towering, stone portico, the rain managed its way to her. It was cold and spitting, and her hair had gone limp a very long time ago, plastered to the sides of her face under her terribly impractical hat. She didn't even bother trying to brush it from her cheeks any longer. The rain would only drive it back.

The rain, however, did not hold back the onlookers. At first, it was only a few stragglers here and there, coming to see what was happening at the new observatory as they passed by to do their shopping and attend to business matters. But it seemed those few robust individuals had soon gone on to spread the word that something was amiss at College Park because soon carriages began to arrive clogging the street.

Alice recognized the crests of the Earl of Bannerbridge and the Marquess of Shoresley. There were a handful of barons and even a viscount. The pavement beneath her was teeming now with onlookers, but they had taken to behavior more closely related to gawking, and Alice couldn't help but feel pleased with herself.

Someone had noticed.

Her efforts that day had not gone unmarked, and while it may not have won unfettered access to the observatory for women, Alice had at least raised awareness of the issue.

She adjusted the weight of the chains along her shoulders and raised her chin, pitching her voice to be heard over the spitting rain. "Women are critical in the advancement of science and deserve equal access to the resources that can propel their research forward. Do not let the gatekeepers of this establishment stop the advancement of science. Give women equal access!"

The crowd gathered at the foot of the steps continued to gawk, their mouths slightly open, but their expressions mostly shrouded in the shadows of their umbrellas.

"Grant equal access to women!" Alice called louder, rattling the chains along her arms. Dear God, they were getting heavy.

It was then that she spotted the helmets of the first bobbies. Her heart sank a little as she had only been at this for less than an hour, but she supposed if the crowd had heard of her exploits, so had the Metropolitan Police. She had expected to be arrested, but she hadn't expected it so soon.

"Excuse me."

Alice looked down, at first thinking someone from the crowd was trying to get her attention but it wasn't that at all. There was some kind of confusion amongst the onlookers, shuffling and rearranging as something came free from the mass.

It was a chain but a different kind than the one Alice held. It was a chain of women, arms linked, forcing itself through the crowd. Alice blinked, attempting to shed the rain drops from her eyelashes that clouded her vision.

But then the women pushed free of the crowd, the chain unspooling at the bottom of the observatory's steps, and Alice could see it for what it was.

Lady Emma Thomas, Viscountess Wetherby, and the women of the Ladies' Scientific Guild stood in a line at the bottom of the steps, effectively blocking the progress of the bobbies Alice had spotted earlier. Alice felt an unfamiliar tug at her heart, her legs weakening momentarily until she remembered she had to hold up the chain she was locked to.

But again, the bobbies finally reached them and ordered the ladies to make way. Only they didn't. Much to Alice's surprise the ladies didn't budge.

"I'm sorry, good man, are you saying we should move?" Lady Wetherby's voice projected over the crowd. "We are harmless, innocent ladies attempting to take shelter with one another from this horrid weather, and you would demand that we leave our safe haven. How cruel you must be."

"I didn't say anything of the sort!" This was from the larger of the two bobbies. "I was only asking you to step aside."

Lady Wetherby tightened her hold on the woman next to her, and Alice realized it was May Greenawalt.

"How dare you!" May said then and made to open the umbrella she held in her hands. Only she fumbled it, and the thing sprang open directly into the bobby's stomach. The man lurched backward, his hands going to his stomach as he let out a groan of surprise. "I'll say!" May cried in mock concern. "You're rather clumsy, aren't you?"

"Get out of my sister's way!" This was from Melanie who stood on the other side of Lady Wetherby. "She is only trying to protect herself from this rain. Do you wish for her to catch a chill and die?" This last word was said with a heavy dramatic cry, and the crowd gasped in response.

The shorter of the two bobbies seemed to finally get hold of his senses and raised a hand. "Now see here—"

Mrs. Muskgrove screamed and ducked her head. "Oh heavens, he's raised a hand to me! I'm only a defenseless woman!"

The crowd vibrated with outrage now, the buzz of conversation turning to a boil of consternation. The poor bobbies didn't seem to know what to do as they stood frozen to the spot, the chain of women untouched before them, Alice still securely on her perch above them.

She took the opportunity to shout again, "I demand equal access for women to this observatory in the name of science!"

"Give the lady what she wants! Stop hurting her!"

Alice was so shocked by this cry she forgot to say anything more. She didn't know who the speaker was, but once said the tide of the crowd turned, cheers shouting up and down the street in her favor.

She couldn't help it. She smiled.

Just as Lord Dalton appeared on the pavement at her feet with a gentleman who looked terribly like an inspector for the police.

Oh drat.

She gripped her chain more tightly as Lord Dalton approached Lady Wetherby.

"Dalton, how good of you to come. These bobbies are assaulting us," she said without preamble, her voice watery as though she were truly offended.

"Out of my way, Lady Wetherby," Lord Dalton grumbled. "Don't think I don't know what's going on here."

Lady Wetherby gasped theatrically. "Lord Dalton, I would not expect such crass behavior from you. These bobbies have inflicted pain on me and my friends when all we were trying to do is shelter one another from this putrid weather."

Lord Dalton was having none of it though and pushed his way directly through the line, shoving Lady Wetherby aside. Melanie caught her before she could fall to the ground, but Alice watched, her anger simmering, her determination raging.

"You!" Lord Dalton spat, taking the stone steps two at a time, the inspector stumbling along behind him. "I should have known. Alice Atwood, wasn't it? Arrest her!" This last part was directed at the inspector.

The poor man was a rather bent fellow likely owing to his unspeakable height, and he wore a tattered great coat slick with rain. He fumbled around in his pockets before spreading his hands uselessly before him.

"I'm sorry, my lord. It's just that she's...well, she's chained to the door, my lord." The man's voice wobbled as much as his hands did, and Alice felt a pang of sympathy for the poor fellow.

"Do you think I can't see that?"

"But, my lord." The inspector slid Alice a worried glance. "How am I to arrest her if she's chained to the door?"

Lord Dalton's nostril flared. "I don't care how you do it as long as you do it, you incompetent fool!" He spat the last word, his fists waving wildly in the air.

Alice tried very hard to hide her smile by lifting her chin, letting the rain wash her hair back from her face.

The poor inspector looked between her and Lord Dalton before finally stepping forward. The moment he laid a tentative hand on her arm another voice came from the crowd below.

"Lord Dalton, is there a problem?" The voice was cool, calm, measured, and Lord Dalton turned just as the man came up the last step and joined their odd tableau in front of the observatory.

"Lord Knighton." Dalton shook a finger in Alice's direction. "This chit seems to think she can stage a protest at our fine establishment, but don't worry. I've brought the police to see it's taken care of. You mustn't worry."

"No, of course not, Dalton," Ransom said, his voice still even and cool. "But Inspector, I would suggest you remove your hand from my wife or risk the weight of the peerage coming down on you."

Alice did smile then. She always did when Ransom referred to her as his wife. They had been married for all of three days, and she wondered if she would ever grow used to it. Being married to this man. This man who supported her, believed in her, loved her.

"Your wife?" Dalton had lost his bravado, his anger replaced by insipid fear. "Knighton, you can't mean—"

"I do." He took a threatening step toward the poor inspector. "Now if you don't remove your hand—"

The man snatched back his hand so quickly he fell off the top step. He caught himself before careening down the rest of them though, and Alice breathed a sigh of relief. It wasn't the inspector's fault what was happening there, and she didn't wish to see him hurt.

Ransom stood between her and Lord Dalton now, and Alice peered around his shoulder. She wanted to see Dalton's face for this next bit.

"Lord Dalton, it seems there's been a misunderstanding obviously. You wouldn't wish to have a countess arrested, would you?"

Dalton wiped the rain drops from his forehead, and Alice noticed how the man's hand shook ever so slightly. "Of course not, Knighton. I shouldn't do anything of the sort. Please accept my apologies."

Ransom looked over his shoulder at her, and she pressed her lips together to keep from smiling. It was rather difficult to arrest a member of the peerage, and Ransom had been correct. Lord Dalton wouldn't have thought twice to arrest the impoverished daughter of an earl, but a countess was a different matter entirely.

"There's one other thing that I should like to discuss with you, Dalton. I'm concerned the limited membership is preventing the observatory from being the true bastion of scholarship I had hoped it would be. I shouldn't like my future donations to be curtailed due to a lack of scholarship here."

Lord Dalton actually stammered. "Of course not, my lord. I think it would be possible to discuss the membership qualifications at the next investors meeting."

Ransom smiled. "That would be most agreeable." He gestured down the stairs. "Now I believe you owe my aunt an apology."

Alice cast her gaze down the steps to where Lady Wetherby stood, arms crossed, chin high. Lord Dalton stammered some more before retracing his steps to the ladies of the Guild.

Ransom turned fully to face her then, his smile soft and knowing as he took a small iron key from his pocket.

"Lady Knighton, whatever are you doing out in this weather?"

Alice wrinkled her nose. "I hadn't counted on the day being quite so dreary, but I'm rather pleased with the turnout. Aren't you?"

She thought he would turn about to see the crowd still gathered at the foot of the steps, but his eyes remained locked on her, that warm, knowing smile still playing at his lips.

"You know the only one I care about here is you, Lady Knighton."

She shivered, and it wasn't from the chilling rain. "I heard rumors of such things, but I—"

"Alice Mary Atwood!"

Alice snapped her lips shut, her eyes frozen on her husband's face as he registered the cry behind them. He shifted in time for Alice to see not one but both of her sisters hurtle themselves through the members of the Ladies' Scientific Guild and up the stairs. They wore traveling cloaks, but the hems of their skirts were soddened and caked with mud, and Alice felt a pang of guilt, wondering how far they had been walking out in this in order to reach her. The street was quite clogged in either direction for some blocks after all, and there was no possible way their carriage could have made it this far.

"Your middle name is Mary? I wouldn't have thought it," Ransom murmured out of the side of his mouth before Adaline reached them. Her height was an advantage to poor Amelia, and she took the stairs two at a time.

Alice hardly had time to reply, "My mother thought it biblical."

He only had time to give a grunt of acknowledgment before Adaline descended.

"Alice, what on earth are you doing?"

Alice tried to reply but just then Amelia reached them and gasped, a sound louder than any noise she had made in the whole of their existence, and Adaline turned a concerned gaze in her direction.

But Amelia was already pointing back at Alice. "Your hair," she gasped again. "What have you done?"

Adaline turned back, and Alice saw the moment her sister took in Alice's hair. Her eyes grew round as did her mouth, but she made no sound.

Alice tried to reach up and touch the short strands, but she couldn't very well let go of the chain or she might collapse. "I cut it," she said, smiling now. "Don't you like it? It's rather more manageable I should say, and it no longer gives me a headache when I'm trying to read." She tried to toss her head to show just how lovely her shorter do was, but the rain had plastered it to her head. She would show them later perhaps.

It was then that three gentlemen broke free of the crowd below, and Alice recognized Ash and Uncle Herman beneath sodden greatcoats, and she realized with a spark of excitement that the third gentleman must be Amelia's husband.

"Is this the Duke of Greyfair?" she said, smiling widely in greeting.

The poor gentleman stopped behind Amelia, putting two reassuring hands to Amelia's shoulders. He gazed at Alice with curious attention and not a small degree of alarm.

"I do beg your pardon, Greyfair. I'm not normally chained to an observatory. I reserve such behavior for special occasions, you see." She couldn't stop smiling, seeing both of her sisters and their husbands back in London. And— "Uncle Herman, where in the name of Zeus have you been?"

Uncle Herman blinked at her, rain drops shedding from his bushy eyebrows. "I went to the Bodleian for a few days. They have some rare texts I wished to study. I thought you had gone with Adaline," he said, pointing to the sister in question.

Who at that moment was glaring at Alice as she said, "And I thought you were staying with Uncle Herman."

Only Amelia's face remained neutral, ever the calming sister.

"Oh, I see," Alice said, adjusting the chain along her shoulders. "Well, I'd be happy to explain once my husband unlocks me from this chain and—"

That was quite the wrong thing to say as not only did Uncle Herman, Adaline, and Amelia burst into exclamations, but Ash did as well. At poor Ransom, who really had nothing to do with this.

"Husband?" Adaline cried, her eyes flying to Ransom, for there was no one else under the portico to whom she could be referring. "Husband? You two are...wed?"

"Alice, what happened?" Amelia stepped forward between Adaline and Ransom. "If you have harmed my sister, I shall do everything in my power as a duchess—"

"He didn't harm me," Alice cut in. "We were wed by special license two days ago. I'm so sorry for the haste. Ransom suggested we do so in order to reduce the threat of arrest when I did this." She held up her arms, sending a cacophony of clanking chain bouncing off the portico stone. "I'm sure we could hold a private ceremony later if you both should wish." She looked to Ransom who was already nodding.

Adaline and Amelia did not look convinced, their expressions and silence stonier than the blocks that made up the observatory at her back.

Finally it was Uncle Herman who said, "My God, Alice, your spectacles. You're not wearing them."

Dear Uncle Herman. How lucky had they been for him to come into their lives?

"No, Uncle, I'm not wearing them because I don't actually need spectacles." This declaration worked to break her sisters' expressions. "You see, I hid behind those spectacles just as I hid behind my hair and those terribly uncomfortable gowns. It was all I could think of to protect myself because I knew I wasn't quite like the other debutantes, and I certainly wasn't what Mother and Father had wanted." She licked her lips. "At least, that's what I believed until someone showed me the truth about who I really was." Here she couldn't help but slide a glance in Ransom's direction. She had only meant to glance at him, but the look on his face captured her attention. There it was again. That look of love, yes, but the one that held everything she had ever sought in her life. Who knew that it was there all along? She had only to find the right person. She turned back to her sisters. "I hope you don't mind terribly if I am just myself now."

Adaline and Amelia wore twin expressions of compassion tinged with sadness, but surprisingly, they also showed understanding and perhaps empathy. For the first time, Alice wondered how her sisters had felt growing up under the pressure of their parents, and if perhaps, it wasn't as rosy as Alice had believed.

Adaline moved first, attempting to wrap Alice in a hug only to be impeded by the chain that still lay across her shoulders. It was practical Amelia who suggested they finally unlock the chains and free Alice so they could get out of this rain.

Ransom set to work, but it soon became apparent that the rain and cold had impaired the lock somehow, and it took all four men to pry the thing loose. As it was, Alice had to wiggle through a hole made large enough by her two brothers-in-law holding the chain open in order to free herself.

The men were still working on removing the last lock Alice had placed on the chains she had wrapped around the iron handles of the front doors of the observatory when Lord Dalton reappeared.

His white mane of hair protruded from under his rain-slicked beaver hat, and she noted his mustaches twitching wildly as though he were muttering something under his breath.

"Lady Knighton, I should like to say something," he said as he approached her.

Alice looked behind her, but Ransom was preoccupied

with the lock as her two brothers-in-law held up the bulk of the heavy chain, attempting to relieve the pressure from the padlock as her uncle supervised, and Adaline and Amelia attempted to keep their husbands from hurting themselves.

She turned back to Lord Dalton. "Yes?"

His mustaches were moving furiously now. "I was right about you," he said, bringing up one finger to point in her direction. "I was right all along. You are *unnatural*."

The word was like a mallet hitting a gong, and somewhere deep inside of her a warning note tolled.

"It was you," she breathed. "You wrote the letter rejecting my work for the Scientific Scholar Society."

"Of course I did. I would never let a female within the hallowed walls of that journal. It is unheard of. It is blasphemy. It is—" His voice had been steadily rising as he laid out the litany of Alice's sins, and it drew the attention of her husband.

She felt it more than saw it. First it was his gaze on her, and then his body turning in her direction. She could feel him coil at her back, ready to spring, but she held up a hand, stopping both her husband's advancement and Lord Dalton's tirade.

"Excuse me, my lord," she said. "But it turns out I do not accept criticism from a person from whom I would not seek guidance." She smiled softly. "Your words are, therefore, meaningless to me." She turned about and plucked the heavy chain from Greyfair and Ash and spun about, dropping the entire thing into Lord Dalton's unsuspecting arms.

He crumpled to the stone floor of the portico, buried under the heavy weight of the chain. His cry of surprise and disgust at finding himself in a puddle rang about said hallowed walls he had coveted so dearly as to keep others from it.

"Good day, Lord Dalton," she said and took her husband's arm as if it were the most natural thing in the world.

* * *

"Do you suppose we must thank him? I hate to think I'm indebted to such a wastrel." Ransom played with the short strands of his wife's hair as she nestled against his shoulder as they lay in the little boat on the pond, gazing up at the stars.

It wasn't raining now as it had been that day on the observatory steps, and the sky was a blanket of stars above them, the boat rocking gently in the night breeze beneath them.

Alice wiggled closer to him, pulling the quilt over them more snuggly. Summer was giving way to autumn, and he would miss these evenings come winter when they couldn't sneak away in the night for the cold.

"I don't suppose we must tell him what part he had to play in all this."

When Alice had finally told him the reasons for kidnapping him for seduction lessons in the first place, Ransom couldn't have said how he felt. His emotions had taken a dive into a kaleidoscope of commotion. He had felt saddened and angry, hurt and confused. He didn't know why she hadn't told him earlier, but then he realized how vulnerable that would have made her, and really, that night in the carriage, he was nothing more than her new brother-in-law's closest friend. How could he have expected her to tell him such precious things?

But she had told him everything now, and for that, he was grateful. Grateful that she trusted him so, that she loved him so, that he could be there to take care of her, yes, but it was more than that. He liked standing behind her, supporting her, celebrating her triumphs. Alice Atwood had made it perfectly clear she didn't need rescuing. She didn't require permission, and she didn't take the criticisms of others lightly. That was what made them partners.

The women of the Ladies' Scientific Guild had been hailed as heroes. All of the newspapers had greatly exaggerated the tales of their heroism, the wrath they had suffered at the hands of the Metropolitan Police, the pillars of community and science that they were. Aunt Emma had reveled in it.

But none had been as exalted as the lady chained to the great doors of that behemoth of scholarship and study. Lady Alice Shepard, the new Countess of Knighton, had become an icon of women's advancement in the field. Journals across England and even some American ones scrambled for her work, wishing to be the first to publish her findings. Alice had, of course, rejected them, directing the journals to the real experts in the respective fields, namely the women of the Ladies' Scientific Guild.

The Guild itself had seen such a surge in membership inquiries as to have Aunt Emma seek space at the observatory itself to host their meetings.

Lord Dalton was only too happy to agree to it.

Ransom couldn't help but smile as the events of the past few weeks tripped through his mind.

Once, he had thought of love as a drowning thing. Something that would have consumed him until he was no longer himself, but that hadn't been the truth. Real love, the kind he had with Alice, was about lifting one up. It only made them stronger to have each other.

"I guess it isn't necessary," he said, pushing back a strand of hair that had fallen along her cheek.

He remembered how he had longed to see her hair down, cascading around her shoulders, and he had felt a pang of apprehension when she had stated her intentions to cut it. He had been entirely wrong. Her gorgeous thick hair now framed her face, showcasing her in a way she never would have allowed before. Every time he saw it, he remembered how far they had come and couldn't help a pang of pride at seeing it.

She was so beautiful, but only he could know just how truly beautiful she was because he knew both her outsides and her insides, her depths and her secrets. Just as she now knew about him.

"Has your mother written from Catanzaro?"

He nodded, taking the opportunity to dip his head into her hair, inhaling the faint scent of lavender from her soap. "She said the trip was uneventful and should we wish to visit, we are welcome at any time."

Alice lifted her head at this and stared down at him. "Truly?"

He nodded. "She seems rather taken with you, I'm afraid. Not that I can blame her."

His wife frowned. "I was rather rude." She wrinkled her nose. "I told your mother to—" Here she mouthed the words *shut* and *up*.

He laughed, the sound disturbing the quiet of the night. "I think it was that moment she felt most alive in thirty years. You tend to have that effect on people."

Not only had his mother retreated to Italy, but Lord Ridgeway had reportedly scampered back to London, terrified by the brazen woman who had confronted him in the middle of a ball no less.

Alice let her eyelids close and moved to drop her head back to his shoulder, but he stopped her with a hand under her chin. "I'm not going to let you hide, Alice Atwood. Not anymore."

Her face was the picture of innocence then. "Who said

anything about hiding?" Her hand moved to his chest where she made a demonstration of undoing one button and then another. "I was merely going to proceed where we had left off in our lessons." When her eyes met his, her look was heated, and his body coiled in response. "As a scientist, I should like to document precisely what kind of affect it is I have on *you*."

"Well, if it's for science." He reached up and pulled her down, her surprised laugh filling the night just before he kissed her.

CHAPTER 16

 *ome months later...*

"I'VE NEVER HOSTED A DINNER PARTY." Uncle Herman straightened his shoulders regally, but it only served to push his bowtie into a lopsided tilt.

Alice reached up and smoothed it back into place. "It's only us, Uncle Herman. You have no need to be so nervous."

Uncle Herman's bushy eyebrows traveled to his hairline, and as that had receded quite a ways back on his forehead, it was rather an incredulous expression. "I think that is precisely why I should be nervous."

Ransom raised the glass of whiskey he had just poured for himself in salute. "I'm with you on that point, Uncle Herman."

It was strange seeing her husband in her childhood home. Theirs had been a rather odd courtship, and it was only once he had stepped inside Biggleswade House, and then it had been under rather unusual circumstances. Warmth spread through her at the sight of him now, relaxing against the mantelpiece, glass in hand, as though he had always been a member of the family.

She smiled, unable to stop herself, and Ransom smiled back. She still wasn't used to it. This silent communication that seemed so natural between them, but perhaps that was a side effect of marriage.

Marriage had turned out to be a glorious affair, but even more surprising was how much Ransom took to it. He particularly enjoyed calling her *Wife*, and she was afraid soon she wouldn't respond to anything else, her given name completely forgotten.

Her work kept her busy most days now. Her *work*. It seemed so strange to think of it like that, but she tried to keep it from her mind that evening. Besides she and Kathryn —she'd taken Kathryn with her when she'd married, of course—had everything ready for the next meeting of the Ladies' Scientific Guild, so she needn't worry that night. It was only about enjoying the company of her family.

The sound of the front door opening traveled down the corridor and into the drawing room where they waited. The murmur of voices soon followed and within moments her sisters tumbled through the doorway, their arms locked together. They hadn't bothered to shed their cloaks and hats at the door and upon entering the drawing room they came directly toward Alice, wrapping her in a fierce hug. They brought with them the crisp scent of winter and the lingering scent of smoke fires, and she burrowed into them.

She saw Adaline nearly every week and sometimes more often than that, but Amelia loved her home along the coast, and it was rare they could lure her back into town. They broke apart long enough to gush appropriately over Amelia's rounded stomach. Adaline predicted the babe would be there any day as she usually did, and Alice would correct her that there was a specific gestation period for babies and this one would be no different, and this exchange for whatever reasons always made them laugh.

Alice finally extracted herself from her sisters' embrace to greet their husbands. The Duke of Greyfair had turned out to be a lovely addition to their family, and she went to him first, inquiring as to the development of the lending library he had established in the village nearest his home in Kent.

"It should be operational by next week," he informed her, a broad smile splitting his face.

Ash cut in with a clapped hand to his brother-in-law's shoulder. "You should see it, Alice. I swear the place rivals any libraries of the great universities of England!" he cried before pulling Ransom into a discussion about horses.

Conversation fell into a buzz of separate conversations then as everyone tried to catch up with everyone else while cloaks were removed and hats and gloves passed on to Mrs. Marble who took them back to the hooks in the front hall.

Alice paused suddenly amidst the chaos to drink in the sight of her sisters and Uncle Herman, of her new brothers-in-law and most importantly, her *husband*. Had it been less than a year since they had stood in this room, facing the uncertainty of the future, sure their fates would end in doom?

Look at them now. Each of the Atwood sisters caught up in the vibrancy of their own lives, still coming back to one another, hovering around Uncle Herman who had miraculously come to save them. To make them the kind of family they had never been.

It was several minutes later when the sound of the front door opening cut through their conversation.

Uncle Herman looked around. "We're all here. Who on earth could that be?"

"I hope you don't mind," Ransom said. "But I've invited my aunt to join us."

At his words, Lady Wetherby appeared in the doorway. She wore a simple gown of varying shades of blue that accentuated her height and capped off her ensemble with a wreath of feathers on her head that only served to make her appear like royalty.

"Uncle Herman, may I introduce my aunt, Lady Wetherby?"

Lady Wetherby made to curtsy and stopped, her gaze riveted to the side where a pile of post had gathered on the sideboard. "Is that Downey and Hughes' latest research about their concave telescopes?"

It was a beat before Uncle Herman finally managed, "Yes, it is. Are you familiar with Downey and Hughes?" Her uncle made his way around the room to where the book lay on top of the pile of post. He picked it up, smoothing one hand over the pristine, new leather cover.

"I'm quite familiar," Lady Wetherby said. "My husband was one of their early colleagues."

"You don't say," Uncle Herman intoned, his eyes widening. "Your husband wouldn't be Bart Thomas, the late Lord Wetherby?"

Lady Wetherby smiled, her eyes crinkling in happy memory. "That's him. Did you know him?"

Alice held herself very still, her gaze enraptured. She had never seen her uncle, well, so flustered. He rubbed at his beard, stroking the gray hair like a talisman.

"I had the pleasure of meeting him once at a conference. Intriguing man. I'm so terribly sorry for your loss."

Lady Wetherby smiled and gave a dip of her head in acknowledgment. "We were all lucky to have him for the time we did."

Silence fell then, but Uncle Herman continued to study

Lady Wetherby, and Alice suddenly became aware of how physically matched the pair were. Lady Wetherby's generous height meant Uncle Herman didn't need to look down quite so far.

Finally Lady Wetherby tapped the cover of the book in Uncle Herman's hands. "Perhaps you'd like to discuss this over dinner."

Uncle Herman smiled, but she noticed the way his eyes never dropped to the book. He only saw Lady Wetherby. "That would be wonderful," he said, his voice a near whisper.

Alice turned her head, catching Ransom's eye. Her husband's expression didn't change, but it didn't need to. In his eyes, she saw what she needed to see, and happiness spread through her.

It seemed hope had finally returned to Biggleswade House.

ABOUT THE AUTHOR

Jessie decided to be a writer because there were too many lives she wanted to live to just pick one.

Taking her history degree dangerously, Jessie tells the stories of courageous heroines, the men who dared to love them, and the world that tried to defeat them.

Jessie makes her home in New Hampshire where she lives with her husband and two very opinionated Basset hounds. For more, visit her website at jessieclever.com.